Bex Carter 4:

The Great

"Boy"cott of

Lincoln

Middle

The Great "Boy"cott of Lincoln Middle

Book 4 of the Bex Carter Series

Other books by Tiffany Nicole Smith:

Burkley and the Beasts: The Sea Serpent

Books 1-5 of the Fairylicious Series

<u>The Bex Carter Series</u>

Book 1: Aunt Jeanie's Revenge

Book 2: All's Fair in Love and Math

Book 3: Winter Blunderland

Book 4: The Great "BOY"cott of Lincoln Middle

ISBN: 9781499132915

Cover Designed by Keri Knutson

(Alchemy Book Covers and Designs)

Twisted Spice Publications

For every girl who doesn't always feel beautiful. You are!

I'd love to hear from you!

Twitter: @Tigerlilly79

Facebook: https://www.facebook.com/tiffany.smith.735944

Website: authortiffanynicole.com

Email: authortiffanynicole@gmail.com

Bex Carter: 4

The Great "Boy"cott of Lincoln Middle

Tiffany Nicole Smith

1

The Lincoln Middle School
Insane Asylum
sighs

Apparently, I go to school with a bunch of lunatics. I mean it. Lincoln Middle School can be an actual loony bin. The craziness started that one fateful day in Mrs. Conway's third-period social studies class.

My hands clutched the edges of my desk. Every year, Mrs. Conway makes her eighth-grade social studies classes participate in a Family Living project. The title of the project was actually "How Will I Survive?" and it was designed to get us thinking about our futures. We had to pretend to be married to someone in the class and, as if that wasn't bad enough, we had to take care of a "baby" that was actually a bag of flour. Last year, when I was a seventh-grader, I'd seen the eighth-graders walking around with bags of flour dressed like babies and I was embarrassed for them. I'd prayed that, by some miracle, Mrs. Conway would either do away with that silly assignment or retire. My prayers had not been answered.

She stood in front of the class with her clipboard, reading off pairs of names.

"Please, don't give me a weirdo. Please, don't give me a weirdo," I muttered to myself. My greatest fear was being paired off with a jerk like Brayden Avery or a weirdo like Josh Urchin, who was using scabs from a scrape on his elbow to play tic-tac-toe by himself at that very moment.

"Bex Carter," Mrs. Conway called. I braced myself. This was only a two-week project, but if I got stuck with someone totally annoying, it would seem like two years. "You will be married to Santiago Ortiz."

I breathed a sigh of relief and let go of my desk. Santiago was a good friend of mine, and neither a jerk nor a weirdo. He looked back at me and gave me a thumbs up.

Mrs. Conway finished reading the list of names. I chuckled to myself when Kristen Lee got stuck with Josh Urchin. She totally deserved him. She wasn't quite the meanest girl in school, but she was close to it.

"Okay," Mrs. Conway said, "when I call your name, please come up and claim your baby."

When my turn came, I was informed that I had a girl. I walked over to a table on the side of the room and lifted a bag of flour. It was much heavier than it looked. I was already dreading carrying it around for two weeks.

"I will give you the rest of the class period to decorate your babies," Mrs. Conway said. "Most students put clothes or blankets on their children when they get home, but that's up to you."

Santiago and I went over to the table where Mrs. Conway had various art supplies spread out for us to use.

Santiago grabbed some red yarn. "The baby should have red hair like you," he said, handing me the yarn. I grabbed a pair of brown wiggly eyes that I remembered using for art projects in kindergarten and a pink marker for rosy cheeks. Santiago and I both felt like that was good enough.

"How do you feel about signing a prenuptial agreement?" Santiago asked as we worked.

"What?"

"A prenup, so if we get divorced you don't take all my money. I am rich."

I had no idea how much money Santiago had, but it must have been a small fortune. He was always thinking up some way to charge people for something. He was a technology genius and even had a website design business. Aside from that, he ran a bodyguard rental service to help kids fend off bullies and he was selling real hall passes. It seemed like each week he came up with a new idea. He'd been doing that since we were little. I remembered buying a red crayon from him in the first grade. He always had a box full of perfectly sharpened crayons. If one of yours broke, you could buy one from Santiago for ten cents.

I cut some pieces of red yarn from the spool. "I don't need your money, I'll have my own. And I'm keeping my last name."

"Good," Santiago said.

We glued the red yarn to our flour-baby's head, followed with the wiggly eyes, and then colored her cheeks. I thought she looked pretty cute—for a sack of flour.

Ava Groves stood up in the middle of class and held her bag of flour in the air like Rafiki did with Simba in *The Lion King.*

"I shall name thee Crimson Rain," Ava G. announced. Seriously, those were her exact words. So dramatic.

Ava went by Ava G. because she belonged to a trio of Avas. The others were the blonde Ava T. and the brunette Ava M. The three of them were permanently joined at the hip. Because Ava G. was the most popular girl in school, and my classmates had no minds of their own, they followed suit by giving their babies equally ridiculous names.

"Periwinkle Rose," Ava M. declared; followed by Ava T.'s announcement: "I'm naming my son Sparrow Knight."

"Yellow Daffodil," someone else shouted.

Santiago and I looked at each other. He shrugged. "I've always liked the name Sookie."

"Sookie," I repeated. "I like it. Short and sweet." The truth was we could have named her "Bag of Flour" as far as I was concerned.

"Cool," Santiago said. "Little Sookie Ortiz-Carter."

Mrs. Conway stood in front of the classroom again. "You will have to keep a journal on your experiences with being a spouse and a parent. Please work together and answer the questions thoughtfully. You will only learn from this if you take the situation seriously."

The bell rang and Mrs. Conway dismissed us. I slid my backpack over one shoulder. Santiago and I both stared at the bag of flour.

"Who should take Sookie first?" he asked.

I had no desire to walk around school carrying a bag of flour with red yarn and wiggly eyes glued to it. "I think Sookie needs to bond with her father. She's all yours." I patted Santiago on the back.

9

"Cool," he said, scooping her up. "Don't worry. I'll hand her off to you at lunch time."

"Whatever. Later," I said as I headed to the door. Little did I know that this tiny, innocent project was going to be a major part of the Great Boycott of Lincoln Middle.

2

The Hot/Not List
—feeling annoyed ☹

Later that afternoon, Santiago came over so we could begin
working on our family log. We sat at my Aunt Jeanie's
dining room table, wondering where we should begin. I
lived with my Aunt Jeanie because my father was in jail for
stealing money from his job and my mother had taken off.
We suspected that she was somewhere in Europe.

While Santiago and I discussed who would take care of
Sookie while we were at work, Aunt Jeanie and Mrs.
Groves came from the kitchen holding cups of tea. Mrs.
Groves was Ava G.'s mother and Aunt Jeanie's best friend.
Because they were best friends, they expected Ava and me
to be best friends, but that would never happen. Ava
couldn't stand me and the feeling was mutual. At that
moment, Ava happened to be upstairs in my bedroom
because we were supposed to be having a social
engagement meeting, otherwise known as a playdate. My
aunt and her mother seemed to think that forcing us to hang
out would somehow make us like each other. This
arrangement had been going on for almost two years and
had yet to work.

"Bex, what is that?" Aunt Jeanie asked, narrowing her eyes at Sookie. I guess Sookie did look rather strange.

"Oh, that's Sookie. Our baby," I answered.

She and Mrs. Groves practically spat out their tea. "Your what?" Aunt Jeanie demanded.

"Our baby," I repeated.

"Don't worry," Santiago added. "We got married today."

"What on earth are you talking about?" Mrs. Groves asked.

I explained Mrs. Conway's project to them.

Aunt Jeanie set her teacup on the table. "You're thirteen. What do you need to know about being married and a mother now?"

"It's not like that and it's actually pretty cool if you think about it." He read from the instruction packet that Mrs. Conway had given us. "Middle school students need practical application to experience the ups and downs of finance that plays an integral part of our adult lives. Students will research how much it costs to survive on their own. Students will solve problems based on their careers, family situation, housing, and transportation and manage their finances."

"It's ridiculous," Mrs. Groves chimed in, not impressed.

"They want our children to end up like those girls on that show on the awful TV channel."

I had no idea what she was talking about. In Aunt Jeanie's house, we were only allowed to watch three channels and those three channels showed cartoons 24/7.

"We need to get rid of that project," Mrs. Groves said as the two of them spun on their heels and headed back into the kitchen.

Leave it to those busy bodies. I was sure Principal Radcliff would be getting a phone call the following morning.

Santiago and I completed the questions that we needed to answer about our first day as a family. Before he left, he offered to leave Sookie with me, but I insisted that he have our little one for the first night.

I went upstairs to see what Ava was doing. When I opened the door to my bedroom, I found her standing in front of the full-length mirror Aunt Jeanie had gotten me a few months before because, according to her, a full-length mirror was a necessity for all young ladies. There was nothing strange about Ava standing in front of a mirror. She was the vainest person I knew. What I did find strange was the fact that she was standing there in her *underwear*.

I didn't understand. Maybe Ava was confused and thought she was in her room instead of mine.

I closed the bedroom door behind me. "Ava, what the heck are you doing?"

"Oh, Bex. I didn't hear you come in. Do you think I'm fat?"

I sighed. I didn't have the patience to convince skinny girls that they were skinny. If she was fat, I was an elephant. I wasn't overweight, but I wasn't skinny. I figured this was Ava's way of fishing for a compliment, so I lay on my bed and ignored her.

I started on my science homework while Ava continued to stare at herself, standing on her toes and examining her body from different angles. I'd never seen her act like that before and I really wanted her to put her clothes back on.

"Ava, what is wrong with you?"

13

She finally turned from the mirror. "Brayden and his friends are starting a hot-not list. They're going to be ranking girls by how they look and I'm really worried. What if I don't make the hot list? I'll be humiliated."

A hot-not list? A knot formed in my stomach. If a perfect-looking girl like Ava was worried about this list, where did that leave a normal-looking girl like me?

"I wouldn't worry about it. You'll be fine." Honestly, Ava was gorgeous. She reminded me of Wonder Woman with straight, jet-black hair that ran down her back and clear, emerald-green eyes. Her outsides were the last thing she needed to be worried about. If I were her, I'd be more concerned about my insides. Her personality must look like Godzilla.

When she started to pinch at her non-existent belly bulge, I just had to get out of there. "I'm going downstairs for some ice cream. Want some?"

Finally she grabbed her dress from where it lay on the back of my armchair. "Are you crazy? And ruin my diet?"

"What diet?"

She slipped the dress over her head. "The Avas are on a no-food diet."

"Please tell me that's not what it sounds like."

"We don't eat food food, but we drink plenty of water and fruit juices. I can also eat one fruit a day. This morning I had a tangerine."

"That's not a diet. That's starving yourself." Then I remembered something that had happened earlier at school. "Hey, is that why Ava T. passed out in PE?" Ava T. had fainted in the middle of our volleyball game. It was really scary, but she came to after a minute.

Ava smoothed her dress down in the mirror. "I don't know why that happened. She ate five grapes at lunch."

I just couldn't…Ava was being absolutely ridiculous, but I didn't know what else to say to make her change her mind and realize that what she was doing was crazy. It's not like she would listen to me anyway.

The next day at school, the crazy was kicked up a notch. Kids had gone all out decorating their babies. I saw bags of flour dressed in tutus and others in little suits with bowties. The most ridiculous of all of the ridiculous things was Ava G. She was actually pushing her baby around in one of those fancy strollers celebrities use that cost thousands of dollars.

I stopped by her locker. "Please tell me that you didn't spend a fortune on a stroller for a sack of flour."

"No," she answered. "I borrowed it from my aunt. Nothing but the best for my little Crimson Rain."

I rolled my eyes and went off to find Santiago. He'd said he'd meet me in front of the library with Sookie. It was my day to take care of her. Lucky me.

I found Santiago standing at the library's entrance with a baby carrier.

"Wow," I said, looking into the carrier. "You went all out."

Little Sookie was snuggled into the carrier, wearing a pink-and-white polka-dotted onesie and a head band. She did look kind of cute.

"Good morning, honey," Santiago said, opening his arms and stepping toward me.

I held my hands up. "Santiago, what are you doing?"

"We're married. I was kissing you good morning."

"You will not—*ever* do that!"

"All right. All right. Sookie's been pretty good this morning. If she gets fussy, just rub her back. She likes that," he informed me.

I narrowed my eyes at him. He'd caught the craziness. It must be contagious. "Yeah, sure, Santiago." I grabbed the handle of the baby carrier and lifted it. It was super-heavy. "See you at lunch."

Santiago bent over and gave Sookie a kiss. "Daddy will see you later, Sookie-Wookie," he said in a sickening baby voice. "That's her nickname."

"Right. I gotta go," I said, speeding down the hallway. Santiago was scaring me.

That afternoon, my best friends came over to hang out in my room after my soccer practice. Our babies sat in the middle of the room on my furry rug, having a playdate while we lounged on my super-cool loft bed. Marishca and Chirpy had just come from cheerleading practice and Lily-Rose from band rehearsal. I didn't have many classes with my best friends this year so we tried to hang out as much as possible.

Lily-Rose sat at my vanity table, applying lavender nail polish to her fingernails. "All of you should be locked up. I can't believe you put your babies in your lockers during your practices."

Chirpy was busy examining her face in my hand mirror. "Well, what were we supposed to do, Lily-Rose? Charlie and Oliver wouldn't take them for us because they had basketball practice and they said that was more important than cheerleading."

"Yeah. Boys are scum," Marishca added in her Russian accent. "Oliver's making me do everyzing."

"Not all boys," Lily-Rose argued, carefully pushing her large pink glasses up on her nose. "Maverick is definitely not scum." Maverick was Lily-Rose's boyfriend. They had definitely outlasted the normal shelf life of a middle school romance.

"Santiago's not that bad either," I agreed.

"Not yet," Chirpy said. "Just wait. Their true colors are going to show sooner or later."

Lily-Rose climbed up to my bed and held her hands out to me. "Like it?"

"Yeah, it's pretty," I answered. The color did look nice on her brown skin.

Marishca shook a bottle of hot pink nail polish. "I'll add the flowers now." Marishca was a master at drawing little decorations on fingernails—well for Chirpy and Lily-Rose anyway. I didn't bother with nail polish. It seemed to chip as soon as I put it on. Playing soccer and basketball everyday didn't help either.

"I'm thinking about getting contacts before this not-hot list comes out," Lily-Rose said as Marishca focused on decorating her nails. "These glasses are only going to bring my score down."

"How are you going to put in contacts? You've always said zat you could not touch your eye," Marishca reminded her.

Lily-Rose shrugged. "I know, but maybe I just need to get over that."

"Lily-Rose, your glasses are fine," I assured her. I meant that. They actually suited her face.

"That's not what Jacob said," Lily-Rose replied. She had been paired up with Jacob Lansing who hung out with Brayden Avery and was just as big a jerk. "He said he doesn't want a wife with four eyes."

I shook my head. "What? He wears glasses!"

Lily-Rose shrugged. "I told him that, but he said it's different because I'm a girl."

"My nose is huge," Chirpy whined. The three of us looked at her, still poking at her face in the mirror.

"Chirpy, you've always known that," I told her. "You said you loved your nose because it gave your face character. Why don't you like it now?" I asked. Her nose was the reason we'd started calling her Chirpy in the first grade. It looked like a bird's beak.

"Because Harvey Rosen told her she needed a nose job," Lily-Rose answered for Chirpy.

I was getting madder by the second. "Harvey Rosen who has more craters on his face than the moon? Where does he get off talking about your nose like he's perfect? These boys are out of control!"

Chirpy finally put the mirror down. "I don't know what you're worried about. You'll be on the hot list. My mother says you're an early bloomer."

I looked down at my chest and crossed my arms over it. "Your mother talks about my...bloomings?"

"What, Bex? It's a good zing," Marishca said.

"Yeah, you need to share some of that," Lily-Rose added.

I hugged myself tighter.

"I have no curves whatsoever," Lily-Rose said.

Marishca started on Lily-Rose's other hand. "Me eizer."

"Me either," Chirpy chimed in. "And on top of that, my nose is *huge.*"

My friends were all the opposite of me. While I was super-tall and big-boned, they were short and skinny. Usually I was the one who admired their physiques, especially when people called me "Big Bex" or "Big Red". When I started at Lincoln Middle last year, I was no longer the biggest kid in school and I realized that my size came in handy for sports. Since then, I'd embraced my size. My friends had never been this insecure about themselves and I didn't like it one bit.

Chirpy hopped off my bed and went over to my full-length mirror. "You know, after cheerleading practice, Ava G. was telling us about a diet she and the Avas were on. Maybe we should all try it."

I sighed and buried my face in my hands. Tell me this was not happening.

3

Girl Power

—feeling empowered ☺

After my friends left, I called Ava immediately. Once she picked up, I didn't even give her the chance to say hello.

"How dare you tell my friends about that horrible diet you're on?" I yelled into the phone.

"What?" Ava asked, sounding completely out of breath.

"What are you doing?"

"I was on the treadmill. Do you know that I've gained a half a pound since last week? A half a pound! This diet is so not working."

"Yeah, that's because it's not a real diet and starving yourself is never good for anything."

Ava was silent for a moment and then she began to blubber like a baby. "But the list is coming out and I have to be absolutely perfect!"

There was a good chance I was going to regret the next thing I said, but I said it anyway. "Ava, relax. I'm coming over."

I found Aunt Jeanie yelling at the gardener in the backyard. He seemed to be ignoring her as he continued to wipe his brow and pull weeds.

"Aunt Jeanie, I thought you were going to call Principal Radcliff about stopping the "Family Living" project."

She continued to watch the gardener. "What? Oh, we figured it's not that big a deal. It might teach you something."

Great, the one time I wanted to her to complain about something, she wouldn't. "Anyway, can you give me a ride?" I asked.

It didn't take much to convince Aunt Jeanie to give me a ride to Ava G.'s. When I'd asked, she'd practically thrown me in the car and high-tailed it to the Groves' residence, going 100 miles per hour. At least that's what it felt like. I thought the car was going to flip as we rounded a corner.

I had told Aunt Jeanie to wait for me. I didn't plan on staying long. There was only so much of Ava G. I could take. Aunt Jeanie went into the living room with Mrs. Groves while I headed up the stairs to Ava's room.

I knocked on the door and waited. There was no answer, so I opened the door and let myself in. I spotted Ava G. lying face down on her bed. She didn't even move as I entered. I sat on the bed next to her.

"Ava, get up."

She didn't move.

I pinched her on her upper arm.

"Ow!" she whined. She shot up from the bed and grabbed her arm. "What is your problem? You can't just come in my room and pinch me."

"I'm sorry, but I need to talk to you. It's about this hot-not list and the way some of the boys have been acting."

"What about it?" she asked, still rubbing her arm.

"Why are we allowing them to do this? They have girls acting crazy and feeling bad about the way they look, when they're perfectly fine. Girls like you, Ava. As long as I've known you, you've bragged about how pretty you were. Now, all of a sudden, you don't like the way you look?"

Ava shrugged. "I'm the most popular girl in school. I have an image to maintain. If I get a bad rating on Brayden's list, it could ruin everything. Besides, Brayden and I had a nasty breakup, so I know he's going to be extra hard on me."

A few weeks ago Ava had dumped Brayden in the cafeteria in front of everyone. I thought a public breakup was cruel, but I didn't expect anything more from Ava. As mean as Brayden could be, that day I'd felt really sorry for him. He looked like he wanted to hide under a rock.

"Okay, but why are you giving him that power? Why would any of us girls pay any attention to that list and care about what it says?"

Ava wrapped a thread from her comforter around her finger. "Because it determines who's hot and who's not. Nobody wants to be on the not list."

"So, we're going to let Brayden Avery and his band of idiots determine who's worthy and who's not? Who are they?"

Ava thought for a moment. "You're right, Bex."

"Of course, I am."

Ava frowned. "But how can we stop it? Brayden already has his mind made up."

"We can make him stop by going on strike. He won't have a choice but to stop with his list."

Ava looked extremely interested. "How would we go on strike?"

I had no idea. I was totally making this up as I went along. "Well, we have to come up with our conditions. Brayden has to stop his list or we will take action. Every girl who's going out with an eighth-grade guy will dump him. We won't talk to them outside of our project for Mrs. Conway's class. We won't dress all cute anymore. We will pretty much act like they don't exist."

Ava shook her head. "That sounds great, but how are we going to get everyone to go along with this?"

I pointed at her. "You. You are going to get the girls to go along with this. You're the Queen Bee, Ava." It physically hurt me to sit there and boost her ego, but I knew it needed to be done to get her to see my point.

"These girls do everything you say. Think about the other day when you named your baby Crimson Rain. Everyone started giving their babies ridiculous names right away."

Ava's mouth fell open. "My daughter's name is not ridiculous."

"Yes, it is, but that's beside the point. Ava, you can be a hero to these girls. You have the power to get them to do anything. Use it for good."

Ava beamed. "You're right. I do have a lot of influence over them."

"Yeah. Text everyone and have them spread the word to all the eighth-grade girls. We'll meet in the courtyard before school and tell them our plan."

"Okay, sounds good." Her eyes lit up. "How about instead of a strike, we call it a *boy*cott?"

"I like that. I like it a lot. I gotta go." I left her bed and headed for the door. I took a deep breath and braced myself. It was going to take a lot for me to say this. "Ava, you know you're beautiful, right?" I asked, still facing the door. "I mean, there are girls who would kill to look like you."

"Really?"

I turned to look at her. I'd expected a "duh" or an "I know," but she looked unsure.

"Yeah, really."

She gave me a small smile. "Thanks, Bex." I guess even pretty girls felt insecure from time to time.

The next day at school a huge mob of girls had assembled in the courtyard. I knew we would have to make our meeting quick before Principal Radcliff came to break it up.

I placed Sookie in her carrier on the picnic table and waited. The huddle of girls talked excitedly to one another. Ava stood on the picnic table with a bullhorn. I wondered where she had gotten it.

"Shut up!" she screamed. Okay, not a good way to start a meeting, but the girls fell silent immediately. "Thank you," she said in a calmer voice. "I'm sure by now that most of you have heard about this hot-not list." A small murmur grew as some girls nodded and whispered to their friends. "I say we take a stand against this list. We need to let Brayden and the boys know that we are not going to be judged by them. They need to keep their opinions to themselves and not broadcast them on a blog for all to see. We need to let them know that we will not be embarrassed and humiliated."

"Yeah!" the girls shouted in unison. I had to admit, I was pretty impressed by Ava so far.

"We are going to demand that they cease and desist with this list and if they don't, we are going to *boy*cott!"

"Yeah," the girls said again, but that cheer was less enthusiastic than the last.

"What do you mean boycott?" asked a girl named Carly.

Ava stomped her foot on the picnic table. "If you're going out with a boy in this school—dump him!"

The girls gasped. I knew a lot of them would have a problem with this, particularly Lily-Rose, but I believed in Ava's power of persuasion.

"Yes. I know it sounds drastic, but it needs to be done. Next, we will dress down."

More gasps.

Ava continued. "No makeup. No cute outfits. We will wear sweats to school. Stop trying to impress them. We need to show them that we're not here to be their Barbie dolls. Lastly, we will not talk to them. Obviously, we have to for our project, but other than that, we will ignore them."

I spotted Principal Radcliff walking out of the double doors of the school building. He did not look happy.

"Ava, wrap it up," I whispered.

"Girls, we have to stand united on this. If you're in, shout 'girl power' on the count of three. One, two, three—"

"Girl power!" everyone screamed.

"Young ladies, break this up immediately," Principal Radcliff shouted. The crowd dispersed and Ava hopped down from the table. Principal Radcliff ushered the girls towards the building.

"How did I do?" she asked.

"You were fantastic," I told her.

She smiled for a moment and then her smile dropped. "I'm not sure about this, Bex. I don't think I can run this on my own."

"You don't have to. I'll help you." I'd already established in my mind that I would come up with the ideas and Ava would be the mouth.

"You'll help me? Bex, you and I aren't exactly…you know."

"I know and, for the good of the cause, I propose that we call a temporary truce." I held my hand out and she shook it.

"Truce," she said. The first bell rang and we hurried to class. It was only when I made it to my locker that I remembered that I'd left poor Sookie sitting out on the picnic table. I ran out to get her, but she was gone. I decided then that I would make a terrible mother. Santiago was going to kill me.

I took a deep breath as I entered Mrs. Conway's class. I was immediately relieved when I spotted Sookie sitting on Santiago's desk. The relief disappeared when I saw the look on his face.

I took my seat next to him. "Santiago, I'm so sorry—"

"Really, Bex? Imagine my surprise when I walked up to school this morning and spotted our daughter sitting on a picnic table all by herself. Bex, you abandoned our child."

"I'm sorry. It was only for a minute. I promise. As soon as I realized it, I ran right back out to get her."

"I don't know if I can trust you with her, Bex." Then Mrs. Conway stood at the front of the class so we had to stop talking.

I knew Santiago was angry and he had a right to be, but I felt that he should cut me some slack. This project had only begun a couple of days ago. I wasn't used to carrying around a sack of flour, so it was understandable if I forgot about her. I remembered my mother telling me a story about how she'd left me in the dressing room at the mall when I was a baby. I hoped this wasn't any inclination that I would turn out to be a horrible mother like she was. I might have forgotten Sookie for a second, but I would never flee the country, leaving my children behind.

4

The "BOY"cott
#TeamGirlPower

Bex Carter

Family log entry #1
How has married life been so far?

It's been pretty good. Santiago and I were friends so it's easy because we already know each other and get along great.

Name one positive thing about this experience so far.

You didn't set me up with a weirdo or one of the boys who are being complete jerks.

Name one negative thing about this experience so far.

I made a huge mistake and now Santiago's mad at me. I can't really blame him though.

Ava had met with Brayden to discuss our demands and reported that he'd laughed in her face.

"Should we set the plan into motion?" she asked me.

"Let's wait. Let's wait and see if he actually goes through with his list first," I told her on the phone after school.

The very next day, this appeared on a blog Brayden had started for the sole purpose of this horrible list.

Brayden's Report Cards

Student: Charlotte Hubble
Subjects:
Hair: B
Body: C- Huge Butt!
Face: B
Overall Look: Average
Comments: Charlotte is just okay. She's not pretty, but she's not ugly either. Her butt's too big! Her new name should be Charlotte Hubble-Bubble Butt.
Recommendations: Charlotte should do something to spice up her look and make her butt smaller. I do not know what. It's her job to figure it out.
Hot or Not? I'd have to say Not.

List

Hot	Not
	Charlotte Hubble-Bubble Butt

I read Brayden's blog during free time in computer lab. My jaw hit the ground. I felt horrible for Charlotte. She was a nice, quiet girl who didn't bother anyone and she didn't deserve this. Nobody did. Ava M. slipped me a note to meet Ava G. in the girls' restroom of the 500 wing. I asked for a bathroom pass and went to meet Ava.

She paced back and forth in the empty bathroom. "Can you believe that creep?" she asked as soon as I stepped inside.

I could. Brayden had always been mean.

"I can't believe I actually went out with him!"

I could believe that too. She wasn't any better than he was. I was about to tell her that, but then I remembered we had called a truce.

"Brayden has challenged us, Ava. That means we need to move forward with our boycott."

Ava nodded. "Right."

"We have to start with Operation Dress Down tomorrow. That means no makeup. Sweat shirts and sweat pants."

Ava turned a little pale. I knew this was going to be a huge sacrifice for her. "Yeah. I'll let everyone know."

I had to get back to the computer lab before Mrs. Lindstrom had a fit. She had a strict five-minute policy and she even set a timer the second we left the room for a bathroom break. My time could have already been up. As I raced back to class, I felt a surge of excitement and empowerment. I was going to make Brayden pay for his stupid, demeaning blog.

At lunch we separated ourselves from the boys by eating outside at the picnic tables instead of in the cafeteria. There was a lot of complaining from both sides, but it needed to be done.

"Why are you punishing all of us for what Brayden did?" Maverick demanded. He and Lily-Rose looked like they would shrivel up and die if they didn't get to eat lunch together.

"I'm sorry," I said, pulling Lily-Rose away from him. "Take it up with Brayden. He's the one who started all this."

Maverick sighed and walked away. Lily-Rose watched him as if he were getting ready to board the Titanic.

I put my hand on her shoulder. "It's okay, Lily-Rose. It's for the good of the cause." She gave me a small smile, but I could tell that she wasn't really buying it.

After all the girls settled down at tables with their lunches, Ava took to her bullhorn again. Where did she get that thing and where did she keep it?

"Girls, as of now, no eighth-grade girl is to speak to any eighth-grade boy, except when you have to for class. Tomorrow is Operation Dress Down. No makeup. Everyone is to wear sweatshirts and sweatpants. If Brayden continues with his blog, then we will move on to the next phase. Girls, we are at war and Brayden has launched the first missile, but we will fight back!" The girls applauded and Ava took her seat.

Everyone then started talking about Brayden's blog post, and wondering who his next victim would be.

"I hope he never chooses me," Ava M. said. "I would just die. Poor Charlotte."

I looked around. "Where is Charlotte?"

"In Mrs. Conway's class she asked to go to the nurse's office," Lily-Rose answered. "She never came back. I can't say I blame her."

That made me feel even worse for her and even angrier at Brayden, who suspiciously was nowhere to be seen.

"Hopefully, this boycott will get him to stop and no other girl will have to worry about being Brayden's victim." I tried to sound as confident as possible when I said it, but most of the girls looked like the world was ending. This hot-not list had to stop.

After a fifteen-minute lecture, Santiago handed Sookie over to me. I would be keeping her that night. Once I got home, I promptly handed her off to my little sister and cousins. Surely an eight-year-old and two eleven-year-olds could care for a sack of flour.

"Aww, she's so cute," Penelope cooed.

"Can we make her an outfit?" Priscilla asked.

"Sure. Knock yourself out," I answered. Penelope, Priscilla, and their brother Francois were Aunt Jeanie's triplets. Mostly they were annoying and my sister Reagan wasn't much better.

"Does this mean that I'm an aunt?" Reagan asked.

"I guess so, Ray. I gotta go. Whatever you do, just make sure you don't break her. My teacher will lower my grade."

I left the girls alone so I could do my homework and pick out my bad outfit for the following day. I decided to pick out my outfit first. This wasn't going to be a huge stretch for me.

I liked to dress comfortably, much to Aunt Jeanie's dismay. I only wore dresses and skirts when she made me. Unlike the other girls in my school, who wore full faces of makeup, I'd just dab on a little lip gloss on days that I actually remembered to do it.

I rummaged through a drawer and pulled out a blue sweatshirt with matching blue sweatpants. A plus to wearing this outfit was the fact the Principal Radcliff kept the temperature of our school at -5°. No makeup and my hair would be a thick, curly mess, as usual. My work was done.

The phone rang in the hallway. Ray called out that it was for me. I was the only kid I knew who didn't have a cell phone so I had to take my phone conversations in the hallway where I had absolutely no privacy. It was Santiago. I froze for a minute, remembering that I wasn't supposed to be talking to him.

"Santiago, I can only talk to you about our project."

"Yeah, I know. I was just calling to check on Sookie."

"Why? Don't you trust me?"

"Not with Sookie," Santiago answered without missing a beat.

"She's fine," I muttered.

"What is she doing?"

I rolled my eyes. "What do you mean 'what is she doing?' She's a bag of flour. She's not doing anything."

"You know what I mean."

I sighed. "My cousins and sister are watching her, okay?"

"What? You let little kids take care of our baby?"

I couldn't take it anymore. "Bye, Santiago," I said, before hanging up the phone. We were only three days into this project and I wasn't sure if I would be able to take another week and a half.

5

Operation Dress Down
—frustrated ☹

Santiago Ortiz

Family log entry #1
How has married life been so far?
Bex is cool. We see eye to eye on most things, but now she's not talking to me for no reason. I didn't do anything wrong! I asked my dad about it and he said, "Welcome to married life, son."

Name one positive thing about this experience so far.
I came up with a great idea to make some money.

Name one negative thing about this experience so far.

Bex left Sookie sitting outside all alone. The worst part is that she's not even sorry about it. I don't think she's taking this project seriously. Also, she and the other girls are acting all crazy because of this blog thing.

Getting dressed for school was quick and easy when you didn't have to worry about how you looked.

I stepped into the main corridor with Sookie in tow, ready to see my fellow girls standing strong in unison against Brayden's awful blog. Imagine my surprise when I witnessed just the opposite. The girls were dressed *better* than usual. Party dresses, high heels, hair perfectly curled, makeup galore—the hallway looked like a fashion show. I looked down at my sweats and felt like a total bum.

I headed to the bathroom where I knew the Avas hung out every morning, perfecting themselves in the mirror. Maybe I had gotten the date wrong or something, but I was sure I hadn't.

I heard the buzz of girls chatting before I even entered the bathroom. Once I stepped inside, the restroom fell silent and all eyes were on me.

"Wow, Bex," Ava G. said. She wore a pink party dress with a tutu skirt and silver heels. "I didn't think your look could get any worse." The other Avas snickered.

"What are you talking about? This was part of the plan. We were all supposed to dress this way. The point was to show the guys that we're not just here for their visual amusement. You guys all look better than you do every other day. What's the deal?"

A girl named Cassie stepped toward me. "Look, Bex, it was a great idea, but with this blog, none of us wanted to take the risk of being Brayden's next victim. Poor Charlotte is just traumatized."

I looked at Ava. "Really? I thought you were serious about this."

She looked a little guilty. "I am, Bex. I tried, but I just couldn't come to school in sweats. Cassie's right. Now's not the time to be uglying ourselves up."

"You guys have just set this movement back a hundred years!" I yelled.

Ava T. rolled her heavily made-up eyes at me. "Bex, you are being way too dramatic."

I couldn't take it. I rushed out of the bathroom before I said something I would regret. If Brayden was looking to find his next victim, I would be a sitting duck.

In Mrs. Conway's class, I plopped Sookie down on Santiago's desk.

"Whoa, you look bad," he said. I shot him a look. He cleared his throat and sat up straighter. "I mean, you look...tired. Did Sookie keep you up last night?"

I buried my face in my hands. "Santiago, how would she keep me up all night?"

He shrugged. "Why do you look like that then?"

I explained to him how it was part of our boycott. "Stupid boys. This is all your fault."

Santiago threw his hands up. "Hey, it's not all of us. I think this blog is a bad idea."

I softened. Santiago was right. I shouldn't be blaming every boy for what one boy was doing. "I'm sorry for snapping at you."

"Aww, it's okay honey."

"Do not call me that!"

There was a minute left before Mrs. Conway's class began. Suddenly everyone reached into their pockets or backpacks at the same time. The kids around me looked at their cell phones, which meant that they had received a text. Santiago fished his phone out of his pocket. Before I could ask him what was going on, Mrs. Conway took to the front of the class.

"When I call your name, bring up your homework assignment," she called.

I looked over at Santiago. He was frowning. Why didn't I have a cell phone? I leaned over to ask him what the text said.

"Bex Carter!"

I jumped and looked up at Mrs. Conway. "I wasn't doing anything." It was a reflex. She and my language arts teacher, Ms. Henry, gave me more detentions than anyone.

She narrowed her dark eyes at me. "No, you're not doing anything, but you should be bringing up your homework as I asked. " A few kids giggled.

My cheeks warmed. "Oh." I scooted from my seat to hand her my paper.

Mrs. Conway continued to call names. I leaned over toward Santiago again. "What's going on?"

"Brayden rated another girl on his blog. This one is brutal."

A lump formed in my throat. "Who is it?"

Just as Santiago opened his mouth to answer me, Mrs. Conway yelled for everyone to turn their phones off and put them away.

"You all know better than that. I'd hate to confiscate your phones, but I will if I have to."

Santiago slid his phone back into his pocket.

"Who?" I mouthed to him.

He shrugged.

"Bex Carter!" Mrs. Conway shouted.

"I turned in my homework already."

"Yes, you did. But I just asked you to read the first paragraph on page 112."

More giggles.

I opened my social studies book to page 112 and read aloud, but my mind was wandering the whole time. I prayed that I wasn't the victim of today's blog post.

Serena Simpson. She was the topic of Brayden's blog post and he'd raked her across the coals. Her report card looked like this:

Student: Serena Simpson
Subjects:
Hair: D
Body: F

Face: D

Overall Look: F for fat

Comments: Let's be honest; Serena is fat. Her hair is stringy and her face is just not that pretty.

Recommendations: Diet and exercise

Hot or Not? Definitely Not!!!

Hot	Not
	Charlotte Hubble-Bubble Butt
	Serena BLIMPson (Ha ha!)

I was humiliated for Serena. I didn't know much about her, but I knew who she was. She was in my PE class. She already had it bad enough with the other girls picking on her. She was one of the girls who changed clothes in the shower so no one would make fun of her. I could only imagine how she felt.

At lunch Ava was livid, which surprised me. She hadn't been the one who'd been judged, but she still cared. Maybe there was a heart somewhere in her after all.

The eighth-grade girls gathered outside with our lunches and waited for Ava's response to Brayden's blog post. Serena was there also, looking incredibly sad.

"Bex, you were right," Chirpy said. "This is out of control. The boys in my third-period class were actually reading and laughing at Brayden's post. How can they be so cruel?"

Marishca and Lily-Rose nodded in agreement.

"Girls," Ava began, "what happened today was a travesty. We gave Brayden fair warning. Now it's time to fight fire with fire."

"Yeah!" we all chanted.

"We are not going to take this disrespect anymore!"

"Yeah!"

"We will not be objectified!"

"Yeah!"

"As of tomorrow, I'll be turning the tables. I'm starting my own blog where I'll rate the boys!"

"Yeah!" the girls screamed even louder.

"Wait! No!" I grabbed Ava and pulled her away from the group. "Ava, what Brayden is doing is wrong. We can't turn around and do the same thing. We'll be just as bad as they are."

"Bex, sometimes when people fight dirty, the only way to beat them is to fight dirty too. They'll never understand how bad it feels to be judged like this until they experience it themselves. Trust me. This has to be done."

That evening, my friends and I were hanging out in my bedroom.

"I can't wait until tomorrow," Lily-Rose said.

"Me eizer," Marishca agreed. "Who do you think Ava's going to choose?"

"I wish it could be Brayden," Chirpy said, "but, unfortunately, he's perfect—on the outside anyway."

I tossed my soccer ball from hand to hand. "I think this is a horrible idea. All it's going to do is hurt more feelings. What good is that going to do?"

Lily-Rose pushed her glasses up on her face. "I don't know, Bex, but these boys need a taste of their own medicine. The boys have gotten meaner since Brayden started the list. I can't take much more of Jacob. I seriously want a divorce."

"I know some of them are behaving very badly, but not all of them. What about Maverick, Santiago, and Jeeves? They haven't been acting any differently."

Chirpy shook her head. "*Yet*, Bex. They're boys. They'll side with the others before they side with us. I'm telling you, once Ava starts her blog, it's going to be an all-out war."

I was surprised that the girls were actually keeping up their boycott conditions and not speaking with their boyfriends, especially Lily-Rose. I knew it was a huge sacrifice for them.

I rolled the soccer ball away from me. "I don't want this to turn uglier than it needs to be. We just need Brayden to stop his blog, that's all."

My friends looked at each other and then looked at me. Chirpy grabbed my soccer ball and balanced it on her index finger. "Bex, you wanted us to take a stand and we have. Now we have to take all that comes with it."

I didn't like the sound of that and for good reason.

6

Ava's Blog
#payback

Family Living Journal

Bex Carter and Santiago Ortiz
Where will your family live?

I want to live in a mansion, but Bex wants to live in some kind of loft thing that overlooks the city. We are compromising by buying a small house with five bedrooms, an office, a gym, a playroom for Sookie, a pool, and a basketball court. Bex still thought that was too big at first, but she changed her mind.

—I did not but Santiago wrote in pen so I couldn't change it! - Bex

Ava announced that her blog was scheduled to be released at noon and she refused to tell anyone whom she had chosen to feature. She told us we'd just have to wait.

Brayden hadn't updated his blog yet. Perhaps he was waiting to see what Ava's blog post would be like. The morning went along normally, except for the fact that the girls weren't talking to the boys and the boys were roaming the hallways saying stupid things like, "Who's going to be next?" or "Ugly girls, beware!" The fact that they were walking around so cocky and sure about themselves while we were biting our nails and worrying about this blog made me even angrier.

I'd said about three words to Santiago in Mrs. Conway's class. I felt guilty about that, but it was for the good of the cause.

As I left my science class and headed for PE, I heard someone wailing, "Nooooo! My baby! My baby!"

I followed the commotion. Paisley Thomas stood in the middle of the hallway, staring at a pile of white powder on the floor.

"What happened?" I asked her.

"Someone pushed me! I dropped her and she just burst open!"

"Aww, poor…what was her name?"

"Rainbow Destiny"

Oh, brother. That sounded like a character from *My Little Pony.*

I put my hand on Paisley's shoulder. "Poor Rainbow Destiny, but look on the bright side. She's in a better place." I chuckled because I couldn't help myself. "That big bakery in the sky."

Paisley gasped. "Bex Carter, this isn't funny!"

When I tell you she was crying, I mean really crying as in tears streaming down her face.

"Paisley, come on. She was just a sack of flour."

Paisley brushed my hand off her shoulder. "No, she wasn't. She was my child. As a mother, you should understand." Then she ran through the hallway sobbing and everyone looked at me like I had done something wrong.

"What? What's wrong with you people? It was just a sack of flour!"

Kids shook their heads and walked away murmuring things about me. Sure, make me the bad guy.

During lunch several of us huddled over Ava's pink tablet as she brought up her blog. The screen turned pink and the words "Ava Says" popped up in yellow bubble letters. My heart dropped as I read the post to myself as Ava read it aloud.

Today's topic: Chicken Legs and Bird Chests
Ava says the five boys with the best (and by best I mean worst) chicken legs are: Harold Charles, Dustin Miller, Eugene Garcia, Matt Shepard, and Walter Burns.

Ava says the five boys with the skinniest bird chests are: Harold Charles (congratulations, Harold, on your double win!), Claude St. James, Mikey Gillis, Leonard Thomas, and Aiden Davis.

Ava says: Get to the gym and work out! Tomorrow I will be featuring the boys with the worst skin—gross!

An animated chicken scrolled across the bottom of the page. It would have been cute if it wasn't there to be mean.

45

I felt awful. Walter Burns was my friend Jeeve's real name and he didn't deserve to be made fun of like that. The guys on the list were all pretty nice people. The mean guys who should have been on the list weren't.

I looked around me and quickly discovered that I was alone in my feelings. The girls were cracking up and Ava seemed very pleased with herself. She and the other Avas went back to eating their salads. At least they were eating more than a few grapes.

I didn't think there was much I could do at that point, so for once I kept my big mouth shut.

On my way to soccer practice, I came across Santiago in the hallway talking on his cell phone. Sookie sat next to him in her baby carrier. I was slightly annoyed by the fact that it was my night to take her. Santiago said, "Goodbye," and put the phone in his pocket as I approached. He did not look happy. "That was Brett Henderson."

"Brett Henderson?"

"Yeah, he's married to Paisley. He said you really upset her today."

"What?"

"Someone made her drop Rainbow Destiny and you joked and laughed about it. How would you feel if we lost Sookie?"

I closed my eyes and massaged my temples. That's what Aunt Jeanie always did when she was stressed out.

"Santiago, it's a *sack of flour*. Mrs. Conway will drop them down a letter grade and give them another sack of flour. It's not a big deal."

Santiago looked at me like I was pure evil. "Is that how you feel about Sookie? That she can just be replaced with another sack of flour?"

"Yes, Santiago, because she can."

"Listen, Bex. You need to apologize to Paisley tomorrow and change your attitude. Brett buys a ton of hall passes from me and I need to stay on his good side. If you're going to be my wife, I can't have you embarrassing me like that."

I grabbed Sookie, AKA, the sack of flour. "I'm going to go to soccer practice and act like this conversation did not happen. Later, Santiago." I figured it would be best to remove myself from the situation before Santiago and I ended up not being friends anymore.

As I neared the gym, I spotted Jeeves walking toward the band room with his shoulders slumped. Even though I wasn't supposed to talk to him, he was my friend and I needed to make sure he was all right.

"Hey, Jeeves!" I called, running toward him.

"Hey, Bex," he muttered. His brown hair was usually slicked back, but today it was disheveled.

"Are you okay? I'm really sorry about Ava's blog."

"I'm fine, Bex." But obviously, he wasn't. "It's not like she was telling me something I didn't already know."

"Aww, Jeeves come on—"

"It's okay, Bex. I'm late for practice."

I watched him drag himself into the band room. I had to do something to stop these blogs.

"I tried to tell you," Chirpy said on the phone that night after I'd told her about my run-in with Santiago in the hallway. "He may be our friend, but he's a boy first."

"I know, but he's never acted like that before. He was bossing me around like he was my father or something."

I heard Chirpy smacking on something on her end. I wondered what she was eating. "My mom says that men will try to control you if you let them. I think that was part of the reason she and Dad got divorced."

"I don't know about that. Uncle Bob definitely doesn't control Aunt Jeanie. She does the controlling."

"Well, your Aunt Jeanie is a special case."

We talked about Ava's blog. I told them about my talk with Jeeves. He was very sensitive and, although he kept telling me that he was okay, I knew that he wasn't.

"I feel bad for Jeeves," Chirpy agreed. "I heard that Brayden was livid about Ava's blog. You can bet your bottom dollar that he's going to be extra vicious in his blog post tomorrow."

I hoped Chirpy wasn't right about that, but boy was she ever.

7

The Casualties of War
hides in fear

Bex Carter

How will you and your spouse split the child care responsibilities?

Santiago will work from home so he can wake Sookie up, make her breakfast, take her to school, pick her up, help her do her homework, make dinner, give her a bath, and put her to bed. I will be traveling the world as an award-winning photojournalist. I'll help out when I can.
I did not o.k. this!

The next day in school, everyone was buzzing about the blog posts. Ava's looked like this:

Worst skin (by worst I mean grotesque, lumpy, bumpy, and almost monster-like: Terrence Clay (AKA pusface) and Crater-Face Harvey (Harvey Rosen). Please see me. I can give you the number to my family's dermatologist.

Underneath that, a frog covered with warts hopped across the screen. Ava's blog was bad, but Brayden was really pushing the envelope with his post:

Student: Ava Taylor (AKA Ava T.)
Subjects:
Hair: C
Body: C
Face: C
Overall Look: Average
Hot or Not? Not
Comments: People think she's pretty, but I say she's overrated, average at best. She could lose 5 or 10 pounds.
Recommendations: Get a makeover

<u>Hot</u>	<u>Not</u>
	Charlotte Hubble-Bubble Butt
	Serena BLIMPson
	Ava Try-to-lose-ten-pounds

She could lose five or ten pounds? Great. Say that to the stick-thin girl who's already starving herself. I knew that post was done out of spite. Ava T. was a very pretty girl. If not, Ava G. wouldn't hang out with her. Needless to say, the Avas were furious, and I could only imagine that the posts from this point on were going to get nastier.

"Operation Breakup is in full effect!" Ava announced in the hallway.

All that happened before school began. Mrs. Conway decided to ruin the morning completely with her announcement.

50

"Ladies and gentlemen, may I have your attention, please?" she asked as she closed her attendance book. There was really no need for her to ask us that question. The room was silent, since we were seated next to our pretend spouses and the girls weren't talking to the boys.

Mrs. Conway cleared her throat. "Next Friday we will have a banquet in the gym during fifth and sixth periods to celebrate the end of this assignment." She paused, probably waiting for us to show some excitement, but we looked more like we were sitting in the waiting room at the dentist's office. "Well, doesn't that sound like fun?" Still nothing, except a few headshakes. I felt sorry for her. She had no idea what was going on, but it had nothing to do with her project.

Mrs. Conway shrugged and continued. "Well, anyway, tomorrow I will have all the eighth-graders report to the gym during study hall so that we may plan. I need you to think about what you want to eat. How should we decorate? I will leave that all up to you. After all, entertaining and party planning are all a part of family living." She smiled broadly and clapped her hands. "I can't wait to see what you all come up with!" She looked at us once more and then gave up, shrugging. "All right, take out your social studies books."

I pulled my book from my backpack and looked over at Santiago. He gave me a small smile. I was still a little mad at him about the other day, but I returned the smile. Santiago and I had been friends since the first grade and I didn't want this project or Ava and Brayden's stupid blogs to come between us.

8

Breaking Up is Hard to Do
sighs

Family Living Journal
It's a busy weekend and you both have separate plans. Your babysitter fell through at the last minute. What do you do?

~~Bex will cancel her plans.~~

~~Santiago will cancel his plans.~~

Okay, okay. I'll take one for the team. Bex can go out and I'll stay home with Sookie.

The breakup rule didn't really apply to me since I wasn't going out with anyone, but I was still affected by it. Chirpy, Marishca, and I had spent an hour on the phone the night before listening to Lily-Rose cry about having to break up with Maverick. I'd tried to assure her that it was only temporary and that when the boycott was over, they could go back to being the inseparable MavRose.

Who knew that breaking up with someone could be such a spectacle? Coryn Bailey stood on a cafeteria table during breakfast and broke up with Dylan Andrews, using Ava's bullhorn. Talk about humiliating. One of the cafeteria monitors yelled for Coryn to sit down and be quiet, so she hopped down from the table and handed Ava her bullhorn. Ava used the bullhorn to yell at Brayden. "Brayden Avery, you'd better be glad that I've already broken up with you. I wish I could do it again!" Then the cafeteria monitor confiscated the bullhorn.

Before Mrs. Conway's class, while Mrs. Conway was still outside monitoring the hallway, Sheila O'Brien stood up. "That's it! It's over! We're finished!" she yelled at poor Isaiah Fico as she threw a teddy bear at him. I assumed it was a gift he had given her.

Ava M. used Ava's blog to break up with her boyfriend and Ava T. had the cheerleaders perform a breakup cheer for Bradley Fischer. Needless to say, there were lots of depressed-looking boys walking around. Although it wasn't a pretty sight to see, I hoped that maybe Operation Breakup would persuade Brayden to take his blog down. He wasn't going out with anyone at the moment, so he hadn't gotten dumped, but maybe the other boys could talk him into conceding.

8

Buggin' Out
#grossedout

The following day, all of the eighth-graders met in the gym during study hall. After finding safe places to set our flour-babies, we took seats on the bleachers—the girls sat on one side and the boys sat on the other. Mrs. Conway asked Ava G. to take charge. Teachers always loved Ava because she managed to play the "Perfect Patty" act flawlessly for them.

A few other teachers were there to assist. "Teachers, you are only here to supervise," Mrs. Conway said. "Students, you will plan and conduct everything yourselves." The other teachers seemed fine with this and took seats on bleachers on the opposite side of the gym.

Ava took the floor with her bullhorn. Don't ask me how she'd gotten it back. "All right, guys, this is how this is going to go—"

"FTTTTTTTTT!" Someone had made a fart noise from the top of the bleachers. I looked up. Brayden and a group of boys were laughing hysterically. What were they, five?

Ava rolled her eyes and continued. "We girls will plan everything and the boys will do what we say."

A roar of complaints rose from the boys. Mrs. Conway, who was standing off to the side, looked concerned, but she didn't interfere.

"Yes!" Ava shouted. "We will pick out the food and décor and you guys can do stuff like hang the decorations and carry tables and chairs."

Brayden stood at the top of the bleachers. "That's not fair! You're not going to use us for grunt work!"

"That's the only thing boys are good for!" a girl shouted.

My friend Shyla stood. "Who needs them? We don't even need them for the grunt work. We can do everything ourselves."

"Yeah!" the girls shouted.

Mr. Hawthorne, my pre-algebra teacher, stood. "Hold on, now—"

But Mrs. Conway cut him off. "Mr. Hawthorne, let's let them handle it."

"But—" Mr. Hawthorne objected.

"This is part of the project. When families experience conflict, they have to find a solution. Please let them figure it out," Mrs. Conway said more forcefully.

Mr. Hawthorne didn't look convinced, but he sat back down with the other teachers. Mrs. Conway had a point. I felt like sometimes adults interfered a little too much and that sometimes kids could work things out on their own. I wasn't sure this was one of those times though. Everyone seemed to be getting angrier by the minute.

Just then the ugliest thing I ever saw crawled from underneath the bleachers. It looked like a cross between a spider and a scorpion and was kind of a disgusting brownish green color and the size of a tennis ball. It headed straight toward Ava G. She yelped and hopped out of the way. The strange creature turned around and stopped right in front of the bleachers, as if contemplating what it should do next.

Most of the girls were screaming their heads off. Mr. Hawthorne looked at Mrs. Conway who shook her head.

"Kill it!" Ava ordered.

Johnny McDowell moved forward, but Brayden held him back. "No, if you want to have a boycott, we're going to have a girlcott!

"That's not even a word!" Ava yelled.

Brayden folded his arms across his chest. "I'm making it a word. Kill your own creepy crawlies."

"Fine," Ava said, scowling. "Bex, kill it."

"Why do I have to kill it?"

"You like to do boy stuff."

"Well, I don't like bugs." I looked around at the other girls. There had to be at least one girl who wasn't afraid of that thing. Every last one of them had a look of terror on her face. I looked at Shyla, who I couldn't even imagine being afraid of an ugly insect, but she had turned pale and looked just as frightened as everyone else.

The boys stood back laughing at us. This was stupid. I could see none of the other girls was going to make a move, so I would. I wasn't going to give these boys any satisfaction.

"Somebody, bring me something to catch it in."

Haley O'Brien ran and brought back a small wastebasket. I held it in my hand. The bug, or whatever it was, moved its claws like a crab. I wanted to just throw the wastebasket at it and run away, but that was what the boys expected me to do. I got as close to the creature as I could before dropping the wastebasket on it. Everyone screamed, including me.

"That's great," Brayden said. "You trapped it, now how are you going to get rid of it?"

That was a good question I didn't have an answer for. That thing could have stayed under that wastebasket forever, for all I cared. The basketball team would just have to play around it.

That was when Mr. Hawthorne stepped in to save the day. In one fell swoop, he slid a sheet of paper underneath the upside-down trash can, turned it over, and then grabbed a plastic trash bag and dropped it inside, closing it tightly. I wanted to hug him, but that would have been embarrassing. I mumbled a quiet "Thank you" before he took the bug out of sight.

"Look at that," Jacob said. "A man had to do the job, as always. What was that you were saying about not needing us?"

Ava pointed at Brayden. "I'm going to rip you apart on my blog tomorrow. Just wait."

Brayden threw his hands up and laughed. "What are you going to say? That I'm perfect?" He was the most conceited boy I knew. No wonder he and Ava had gone out for so long.

Ava stepped closer to him and narrowed her eyes. "You know I know something about you that nobody else does."

Brayden's confidence faltered a little and his cocky smile disappeared. What did she have on him? I wanted to know.

"You can't scare Brayden," shouted a boy I didn't know. "Right, Brayden?"

Brayden looked scared to me.

"How dare you make that post about Ava T.," Ava M. said, as she stood next to Ava G. "What gives you the right to judge and nit-pick everything about us girls like you guys are perfect."

"Yeah," Lily-Rose shouted. "Everybody has a flaw so what makes it okay for you to point out ours? Why do you expect girls to be perfect, when you're not?"

"They have a point," I said. "You've had girls in tears over your awful blog. What gives you the right to do that?"

"What about Ava's blog?" Brayden demanded. "You don't think boys have feelings?"

Finally, Mrs. Conway stepped forward, clapping her hands. "Students, I think that's enough planning for one day."

We had accomplished absolutely nothing as far as the banquet was concerned. I actually thought the meeting had set us farther back than when we had begun.

9

Separated

#TeamIndependent

Family Living Journal

You've discovered that you have a surplus of $150.00 in this month's budget. How will you spend it?

I think we should save it for a rainy day, but Bex wants to use it on a trip to the water park. We will compromise, even though Bex got her way the last time.

Fine! We'll save it. I can compromise too. See that, Mrs. Conway?

Brayden released a second blog post that evening, after the big debacle in the gymnasium.
Student: Ava Groves
Hair: A+
Body: A+
Face: A+

Overall Looks: A++++

Comments: Ava Groves is not only the most beautiful girl at Lincoln Middle; she's the most beautiful girl I've ever seen in my life.

Recommendations: None. She's perfect. If I could, I'd give her extra credit.

Hot or Not? Definitely Hot!

<u>Hot</u>	<u>Not</u>
Ava G.	**Charlotte Hubble-Bubble Butt**
	Serena BLIMPson
	Ava Try-to-lose-ten-pounds

I knew exactly what Brayden was doing and he was laying it on way too thick. Ava had something on him. He was using this blog post to butter her up, so she'd decide to keep his secret. Ava was a lot of things, but she was also really smart. I hoped she was smart enough not to fall for this charade.

The next morning, I went to the gym before school. I knew the cheerleaders would be practicing their routines for the basketball game that evening. They always had early morning practices on game days. I found Chirpy and Marischa stretching and Ava sitting on the bleachers, texting.

"Hey. That was some post Brayden made last night, huh?"

Ava looked up from her phone. "Oh, yeah, wasn't that sweet?"

"Ava, you know why he made that post, right? He doesn't want you to make that post you threatened to make yesterday."

Ava looked at her phone again. "Oh, yeah, that. I'm shutting down my blog. I just don't see the point anymore."

"What do you mean, you don't see the point? His posts are awful. He has girls traumatized."

"Yes, but he wrote a very nice post about me. Why should I be mad? Let those girls fight their own battles."

I couldn't believe her. Actually, I could. This was Ava G. we were talking about.

"Ava, Brayden is playing you. He knows you're the leader of this boycott and if he can get you to step down and not care anymore, him and his stupid friends can continue to do whatever they want. Is that what you want? What about what he did to Ava T., your *best friend*? Ava, we need you. These girls will listen to anything you say. I can't do this without you."

Ava looked me in the eye. "I guess you're right. I won't shut down the blog and the boycott is still on."

"Great! Now tell me Brayden's secret." I was dying to know.

Just as Ava opened her mouth, Coach Miranda blew her whistle for practice to begin.

"Gotta go," Ava said as she hit the floor.

I sighed. I would have to find out Brayden's secret some other time.

Later that afternoon, I lay on my bed, completing my science homework. I had to get all my work done so that I could go to the basketball game that evening. The phone in the hallway rang. I was on a roll answering my end-of-chapter questions, so I was a little annoyed by the interruption.

I grabbed the receiver. "Hello?"

"Bex, I need you to get here now," Santiago said.

"What?"

"There's an emergency."

I rolled my eyes, pretty sure there was no emergency. "Just tell me what it is, Santiago."

"I can't. I have to show you when you get here."

"All right, but it better not be something stupid," I answered. I hung up and asked Aunt Jeanie for a ride, thinking there might really be an emergency. Santiago wasn't the type to get dramatic over nothing.

When I got to Santiago's place and entered his bedroom, I was met with the creepiest sight ever: about twenty bags of flour staring at me with their creepy, wiggly eyes. They were on his bed, desk chair, and propped up on the floor.

"Santiago, what's going on?"

"See, you know there's a basketball game tonight, right? Everyone wants to go to the game, but no one wants to take their flour-babies so I opened a flour-babysitting service. At first, I was going to charge $5.00 per flour-baby, but the kids were all, 'Flour-babies don't even move. You're ripping us off.' So I said, 'Okay, three bucks—' "

"Santiago, why am I here?"

"Because, I need your help. I need you to flour-sit while I go to the game."

"How do you know I wasn't going to the game?"

"Are you?" he asked.

"Yeah. I'm going with Lily-Rose. We want to see Marishca and Chirpy cheer."

"Well, you can't go," Santiago said.

"Excuse me," I said, because I knew I had heard him wrong.

"You can't go. Bex, we're married. This is a partnership like Mrs. Conway said. I need you to help me out, partner."

"No."

"What do you mean 'no'?" Santiago asked. "You're the woman. You're supposed to take care of the kids. I'm the man. What I say goes."

I couldn't believe the words that were coming out of his mouth. If this was what marriage was about, I'd stay single forever.

"Chirpy was right. You are all the same. I won't be married to a chauvinistic caveman. Consider us separated!"

"What?"

"You heard me."

Santiago picked Sookie up and held her toward me. "You owe me, Bex. I've been doing all the work, taking care of Sookie. The least you can do is pay me back."

I took Sookie away from him and placed her on his bed. "Santiago, if you want to pretend like she's a real baby and feed her and take her for walks, that's your problem."

He picked Sookie up and cradled her. "You know what your problem is? I was reading about this in a parenting book."

He was reading a parenting book?

"Bex, you're detached. That means you haven't bonded with Sookie. I think it's because of the problems with your own parents, especially your mom taking off and leaving you behind."

My jaw dropped. "How dare you! Don't talk about my parents!"

"Bex—"

"Now I have to go. I have to get ready for the *basketball game*," I said, leaving Santiago's room.

He followed me. "Aww, come on, Bex."

I ran down the stairs. "What about Sookie?" he yelled over the banister.

"You take care of her!" I shouted.

"She needs her mother!"

"She's a sack of flour, Santiago," I said as I raced out the door. I couldn't get out of that house fast enough.

The game was—well…interesting. The girls weren't cheering nearly as well as they usually did. Their cheers seemed stifled and lifeless. I'd seen more energy at a funeral.

During half-time, I walked over to where the cheerleaders sat gulping down Gatorade.

"Hey, what's going on?" I asked Chirpy and Marishca.

Chirpy frowned. "Why should we spend all our energy cheering for those jerks? We kill ourselves at every game getting the crowd hyped up and encouraging the win and what thanks do we get? None. They win and get all the glory."

Unfortunately, we lost to Everest Middle by fifteen points. The cheerleaders didn't look too disappointed. I hoped we could reach some common ground between the girls and the boys soon and then we could once again be a unified student body.

10

My School is Toe-tally Nuts
—feeling guilty ☹

After spending first period completely ignoring Santiago because I had absolutely nothing to say to him (I was really mad this time!), I bumped into Ava G. in the hallway.

"So, Ava, what's the secret? I'm going to burst if you don't tell me."

She led me into a corner next to the water fountain. "Okay, but don't tell anyone. I want them all to be surprised when the post goes live at lunchtime."

"I promise. What is it?"

"During the summer, I went to Brayden's house for a small family pool party. It was the first time I'd ever seen him barefoot."

There was only a minute before the bell rang for our next class. "What, Ava?"

"He's very careful never to take off his socks or shoes in front of anyone—"

"Ava!"

"Bex, on his right foot, he has six toes."

My eyes felt like they were bugging out of my head. "What? No way!"

"Yes. It's not a full-sized toe. It's a tiny one in between his second and middle toe. More like a nub with a nail on it. Bex, it was really gross. I was going to break up with him, but I figured if he kept his shoes on I'd never have to see it."

I couldn't believe it. Not Mr. Perfect. I was expecting something like a hairy mole, but an eleventh toe? The school would have a field day with that.

The bell rang, meaning that Ava and I were both late for our classes. She turned to hurry off, but I grabbed her arm. "Ava, maybe you shouldn't release that blog post."

"Too late. It's scheduled to post automatically."

"I know, but you can stop it."

"I can, but I won't. Hey, I wanted to stop this, Bex, but you were the one who said we needed to stick together and ride this out."

"I did say that, but I was wrong as usual. Ava, please don't do this."

She shook her head. "I can't. I promised Ava T. I'd get him back for what he did to her. Bex, don't worry. Once this secret gets out, he'll be so humiliated, he'll forget about his hot-not list."

During lunch the girls crowded around Ava's tablet, waiting for her blog to be updated. I didn't bother because I already knew what it would say.

At exactly 12:00 on the dot, the group of girls erupted in laughter.

"Ava, is that true?" one girl asked.

"Of course it is. I saw it with my own beautiful, green eyes."

Someone passed the tablet over to me. The title of the blog post read "Toe-Tally Gross!" A giant toe slid back and forth across the bottom of the page. I didn't read anything else.

"What's wrong, Bex?" Marishca asked. "This is great. Brayden's getting a taste of his own medicine."

I could only nod. Marishca was absolutely right. He was getting a taste of his own medicine. I should have felt good about it, but for some reason I didn't.

After school, I rushed to the girls' locker room to get ready for soccer practice. Mrs. Thompson had made me stay fifteen minutes after school for being late to her class. I was really supposed to stay for a half hour, but Mrs. Thompson seemed to have somewhere to go.

After changing, I made my way to the soccer field. I spotted an unusual sight—Brayden sitting on a bench off the side of the field. I knew for a fact that he was supposed to be inside the gym for basketball practice. I had a good idea why he wasn't. All afternoon the talk of the school had been his extra toe. They'd even started calling him E.T.- short for Eleven Toes. Brayden had denied the existence of the extra toe profusely, so naturally the kids demanded to see his bare feet. Of course, he'd refused to take his shoes and socks off, so everyone assumed that Ava was telling the truth. I couldn't help but feel somewhat guilty.

I knew I was already going to have to run laps for being late to practice, so I figured that one more minute wouldn't make a difference. I walked over to Brayden and sat beside him on the bench.

He wiped at his face.

"Are you crying?" I asked.

"No. I'm sweating," he answered quickly.

"From your eyeballs?"

"I'm not crying," he repeated, but the quiver in his voice told me that he was indeed crying.

"Look. I'm sorry about what happened to you today. I'm sure that was humiliating, but you've been humiliating girls all week with your list. It doesn't feel so good, does it?"

Brayden took a deep breath. "You're right. I guess I deserve this."

"You can't help that you were born with an extra toe any more than a girl can help the shape of her nose or the fact that she needs glasses to see, so what gives you the right to make fun of them? Anyway, where do we go from here?"

He shrugged.

"Brayden, all we're doing is going back and forth and hurting each other's feelings. Why can't you shut down your blog and I'm sure Ava will shut hers down."

"I guess," he said, looking down. I resisted the urge to look at his feet.

"Brayden, I think we can do a little better than that. Will you stop making those humiliating posts?"

He sighed. "I won't make another post about any other girls."

I smiled. "Good. I've got to get to practice. I'll see you."

"See ya," he muttered, as I headed off toward the field. I felt like this war might actually be coming to an end.

When I arrived at school the following morning, I spotted a group of girls sitting at a picnic table in the school yard, huddled around Ava.

"Hey, what's up?" I asked as I approached.

The girls had been looking at Ava's tablet, which she quickly flipped over on her lap.

I frowned. "What?"

"Nothing," Ava replied, obviously lying.

"What are you trying to hide from me?"

"Nothing," Ava repeated.

I snatched the tablet away from her. They had been looking at Brayden's blog, the one he'd promised to shut down. When I saw who it was about, my heart fell into my stomach.

Student: Bex Carter (AKA Big Red)
Subjects:
Hair: B
Body: D
Face: B
Overall Look: C
Comments: Kind of cute. Could be cuter if she tried.
Recommendations: Should lose twenty pounds.

Hot	Not
Ava G.	Charlotte Hubble-Bubble-Butt
	Serena BLIMPson
	Ava Try-to-lose-ten-pounds
	Bex Carter (Big Red)

Big Red. I'd been trying to shake that name for years. I was devastated, but I couldn't let the other girls see that. I had been telling them not to care about the things Brayden posted—to ignore them. But now that it was about me, I realized it wasn't that easy. I wanted to crawl under my covers and hide from the world.

My sadness quickly turned to anger. I squeezed Ava's tablet so tightly, I thought it might disintegrate in my hands. She gently pried it away from me.

"Bex, don't worry. We're going to get him back," Ava reassured me.

I nodded and headed for the school building in a trance. Inside, Chirpy, Marishca, and Lily-Rose were waiting by my locker, shooting me sympathetic glances.

"Bex, whatever you want us to do to him, we'll do it," Chirpy said. I knew she meant that. They were the best friends ever.

"It's okay, guys. I'm glad it happened to me and not a more sensitive, insecure girl. Seriously, I can take it." Maybe if I kept telling myself that I would believe it.

In Mrs. Conway's class, I slid as deep into my seat as I possibly could. I so did not want to do this day of school and was contemplating what I could do to get a pass to the nurse's office.

Santiago entered the classroom and plopped Sookie on the table between us. "Good morning."

I folded my arms across my chest and said nothing. We girls were giving the boys an extra cold shoulder.

"Look, Bex, I'm sorry about what Brayden did. That was really messed up. I'm going to tell him to take it down. Not that he'll listen to me, but it's worth a try, right?"

The real reason I was angry with Santiago had nothing to do with the boycott—it was the awful things he had said to me in his house. I continued to stare straight ahead as the bell rang.

Mrs. Conway took to the front of the class. "There are only two more days left of this project, today and tomorrow. Today during study hall, you all will decorate the gym."

Thank goodness. I couldn't wait for this project to be over. I was tired of looking at both Santiago and Sookie.

"Decorations can be found in the auditorium, backstage in the costume and prop closet. I hope you all will figure out a way to work together. We don't need another episode like the other day. That was rather sad. I hoped that through this project you would have learned to communicate and compromise better than that."

After that, my mind began to wonder. I thought about Brayden's comments about me, especially my body. Did I really need to lose twenty pounds? I didn't consider myself overweight, although some mean people- Ava G. included- have called me fat, but I'd never believed that. I was husky, big-boned, and built for sports, but not fat. Or was I?

Decorating the gym during study hall started off horribly. A group of girls and a group of boys had made a mad dash to the prop closet to retrieve the boxes of decorations and then fought over who would carry them back, resulting in two boxes being ripped open and a paper lantern being smashed and stepped on.

Coach Miranda, who was helping Mrs. Conway moderate along with a few other teachers, blew her whistle. "We will have some order here. Brayden Avery, you will be the boy's representative." I knew she'd only picked him because he was one of her favorites, being the star of the basketball team and everything. "As for the girls..." I waited for her to say Ava Groves. "Bex Carter."

I wanted to throw up. If I could blend in with the white walls that surrounded the gym, I would have. The last thing I wanted at that moment was to be a leader. All day I'd felt like everyone had been staring at me thinking, "Hmm, now that Brayden mentioned it, she is fat."

"No thanks," I muttered.

Coach Miranda raised her eyebrows at me. "That wasn't a question."

"Coach Miranda, we both know that I'm not leadership material." She knew that I was a heck of a goalie, but she would have never picked me to be the team captain. Out of everyone, why did she choose me?

"Carter, you may not be the model student, but you are leadership material, believe it or not." Then she turned to the rest of the students, "Take a seat on the bleachers. I want to be able to hear a pin drop." In silent obedience, the kids moved to the bleachers. Just like before, the girls took one side and the boys took the other.

Mrs. Conway took charge. "Take out your notebooks and write this down. You're throwing a surprise dinner party for your spouse. You plan on inviting eight guests

74

and you have a budget of two hundred and fifty dollars. How do you spend it?"

The kids jotted Mrs. Conway's instructions down in their notebooks while Brayden and I moved toward the center of the basketball court and out of everyone's earshot. I had nothing to say to him. I didn't even want to look at him.

"So what do you want to do?" he asked.

Finally, I looked into his eyes, but the last thing I wanted to talk about was decorating the gym. "How could you write that stuff about me? What did I ever do to you? Besides, you told me yesterday that you weren't going to blog anymore."

"I didn't say that. I said I wouldn't blog about any *other* girls and I didn't. I blogged about you. You are the reason everyone knows—*thinks*, that I have an extra toe when I don't. The sixth-graders think I'm an alien."

"How am I the reason? Ava is the only one who knew your secret and she's the one who made the post. You give her a report card painting her as some goddess and then call me fat?"

"Bex, everyone knows your big mouth is the one behind the boycott. You're the one who's getting everyone all riled up. Ava may be the spokesperson, but all this is your fault. She was ready to let things go, but you just had to talk her into making that blog post. I figured I would cut the snake off at the head. Call off this boycott or the next post will be about one of your friends and it will be much worse than the one you got."

"Don't you dare threaten me, *E.T.*" I'd said that much louder than I meant to.

A chorus of "Ooooh," swept across the gym.

"Don't call me that, Fatty," he said before pushing me. It wasn't a hard push. I barely moved, but still, he had no right to put his hands on me.

Jeeves stood from the bleachers. "Hey, don't push a girl!"

"Why not? They don't want us to treat them like girls. Besides, she's bigger than me, so I don't think that rule counts here."

I held my hands up. "It's okay. It's okay. Let's just get started on the decorations. I don't think we need everyone. You should pick five boys and I'll pick five girls to help."

"Fine," Brayden answered and then he called down five of his friends.

I called down Chirpy, Marishca, Lily-Rose, Shyla, and Ava G., since she swore the banquet wouldn't be complete without her finishing touches. She did throw the best parties, so I picked her.

"We *girls* will arrange and decorate the tables while you guys decorate the walls and the bleachers," I said.

Brayden shrugged, "Whatever." Then he and his boys proceeded to make a mess with the streamers.

Mrs. Conway had already arranged for tables to be lined up around the gym so, working together, the girls and I had three tables in place. Ava and Chirpy were busy putting on the tablecloths and making centerpieces when Jacob Lansing decided that it would be a great idea to approach Lily-Rose with their son, Jacob Jr.

"Here. You need to watch him while I blow up some balloons."

"How am I supposed to watch him when I'm moving tables?" Lily-Rose demanded.

"Jacob, there are a hundred other kids sitting in the bleachers. Ask one of them to watch him," I said.

"But I told her to do it." Then he tossed Jacob Jr. at Lily-Rose. She didn't catch him and he landed on her foot.

Everyone in the gym gasped, including Jacob. There's one thing you should know about Lily-Rose: She may be tiny, but her temper is HUGE! Once, in the second grade, a boy named Roger put gum in her hair and—let's just say Roger isn't with us anymore. His family moved to Japan, but before that Lily-Rose had given him a monster wedgie and wiped his face in a mud puddle. It was never a good thing when Lily-Rose got really, really angry.

She picked Jacob Jr. up and dug her fingers into the bag of flour, growling. If I were Jacob, I would have been running, but he stood there looking flabbergasted. The next thing I knew, white powder was running onto the floor because Lily-Rose had ripped the bag open. Poor baby Jacob.

"Look what you did to Jacob Junior!" Jacob shouted. "What's the matter with you?"

"I'll show you what's the matter with me," Lily-Rose yelled back. Then she bent down, picked up a handful of flour, and threw it into Jacob's face. More gasping from the audience. He coughed and spit out the flour that had gone into his mouth. I couldn't help but giggle when I could see nothing but Jacob's eyes.

I knew what he was going to do next. As he knelt to pick up some flour and stood back up, I pushed Lily-Rose out of the way. "NOOOOOOO!" I yelled as Jacob tossed a handful of powder in our direction and it hit me square in the face.

77

I picked up some flour and threw it back at Jacob. Before I knew it, kids were running down from the bleachers and bags of flour were being ripped open and white powder was being thrown all over the place.

The shrill piercing sound of a whistle cut through the air. The flour throwing didn't stop until after four more whistles. The teachers stood on the sidelines in complete shock.

"Everyone freeze!" Mrs. Conway shouted. "Principal Radcliff is on the way."

A sickening feeling landed in my stomach. I wasn't Principal Radcliff's favorite person. We climbed onto the bleachers and waited for Principal Radcliff to come and rail on us. As I sat, I fully took in the mess we had made. The floor, bleachers, and students were covered with white flour. It wasn't going to be a picnic getting this place clean again.

It was so quiet that we could hear Principal Radcliff's footsteps from outside of the gym's double doors. The doors pushed open and he stormed inside and then stopped short. My stomach ached more than it already did.

He looked at the teachers and then he looked at us. He marched across the gym floor, not caring that he was dirtying his perfectly polished black leather shoes with flour.

"What on earth happened here?" he asked us.

Ava G. stood and cleared her throat. "Some of the students, not me, but some of them engaged in a flour-throwing fight." Ava was covered in flour, but the fight had been so hectic, I didn't know if she had thrown flour or not. But I was ninety-nine percent sure she had.

"Thank you, Miss Groves. I would like to know what would possess you all to throw flour. It had to start with something."

Lily-Rose was the first to throw flour and I knew she was about to get into big trouble.

She stood. "I started it," she said bravely. I admired her honesty.

Principal Radcliff looked surprised. Lily-Rose got straight A's and was a member of the band. The only time she'd ever been in trouble was when she had gotten into another fight, but that was only because she had been defending me.

"Why would you do that, Ms. Johnston?"

"Jacob threw a bag of flour on my foot. It really hurt."

"Where's Jacob?" Principal Radcliff asked, scanning the crowd. Jacob raised his hand meekly. He explained to Principal Radcliff the exchange that he and Lily-Rose had had and pretty much how he was being a total jerk.

"B-b-but," Jacob stammered, "it was only because the girls went on strike. This is really their fault."

Principal Radcliff frowned. "Who was the creator of that brilliant idea?" he asked.

"Bex Carter," Ava G. said loudly. "She talked us into it."

I couldn't believe her. I also couldn't believe that the other kids muttered in agreement.

I stood to defend myself. "Why are you guys blaming this whole thing on me?"

"Because you're always behind anything bad that goes on in this school," Ms. Henry snapped.

That was so untrue. I wasn't *always*.

The bell rang for the end of fifth period.

"None of you are going anywhere," Principal Radcliff ordered. "I will have Mr. O'Neil bring over all the cleaning supplies we have." Mr. O'Neil was the school janitor and I was pretty sure he was going to have a heart attack once he saw the mess we'd made. "No one leaves until this gym looks the way it looked before you decided to destroy it. Except for you, Ms. Carter. I'd like to see you in my office."

The other kids sat silently and waited for Mr. O'Neil. I slung my backpack over one shoulder and stepped carefully from the bleachers.

Principal Radcliff told me to dust myself off outside as much as possible. Inside his office he made me sit on a huge towel so I wouldn't get his chair dirty.

It was quiet for a moment as I waited for Principal Radcliff to check his email. The way he looked at me, I was sure he couldn't wait for me to go to high school and be some other principal's problem. Finally he spoke. "Bex, most kids never see the inside of the principal's office, but you—you've been here quite a few times, haven't you?"

"Uhh…maybe once."

"Well, let's see. Last year you started a food fight." Totally wasn't my fault. "Your friends were involved in a physical altercation because they were defending you." That definitely wasn't my fault. "Now, you didn't actually start this flour fight, but you started the boycott that fueled it. What do you have to say for yourself?"

I shrugged. I didn't think anything I said would help me. "You're a man. You wouldn't understand."

"Try me."

I didn't think he would get it, but I told him everything: I told him about Brayden's blog, how the boys had been complete jerks, how they were being extra hard with judging the way girls looked, and how they were being totally controlling and overbearing when it came to our Family Living project.

When Principal Radcliff opened his laptop to take a look at the blog, he turned bright red. "How long has this been up?"

"A little over a week."

He sat back in his chair with his hands folded in front of his mouth. "You're absolutely right to feel the way you do."

I couldn't believe what I had just heard. "Excuse me?"

"Bex, I have three daughters. I know what it's like for girls, especially young teenage girls and self-esteem and self-image issues. Neither Brayden nor Ava should be running those blogs. They will be shut down immediately."

I released a sigh of relief that there wouldn't be any more victims, but the damage had already been done, and I was only speaking for myself. I didn't think I would ever get Brayden's comments out of my head.

"Tomorrow morning I'm going to have a meeting with every boy and girl in the eighth grade. This situation needs to be fixed. I have to say, I'm disappointed in all of you."

"I know. I'm sorry about the flour."

Principal Radcliff took off his glasses and rubbed his eyes. "It's not that. It's the fact that this was going on and none of you bothered to let an adult know. We would have stopped this immediately and saved a lot of hurt feelings."

Yeah, like mine, but he was right. "Sorry," I muttered.

"If something like this happens again, speak up right away."

I nodded and waited for the rest. I needed him to tell me whether he was going to suspend me or if I would have detention for the rest of the year.

"You can go."

I wanted to ask him why he wasn't punishing me or if he had forgotten, but that would have been incredibly stupid. I grabbed my backpack and raced toward the door of his office.

"Oh, Bex," he said, just as I touched the doorknob.

Here it comes. He'd remembered my punishment. I turned to face him. "Yes, Principal Radcliff."

"I commend you for standing up for something you believe in instead of just taking it. Even if the results weren't what you expected."

I grinned. "Thanks, Principal Radcliff."

As I headed back to the gym to help with the clean up, I heard Principal Radcliff announce over the intercom that all eighth-graders were to meet in the auditorium the very next morning.

11

Mirror, Mirror on the Wall
—feeling discouraged ☹

Family Living Journal

Decide where your family will go for summer vacation.

Santiago wants to go to the Bahamas and I want to go to Australia. We will take separate vacations because we are separated.

We had to stay well after school and I'd even missed soccer practice while cleaning up the gym. At home I tried to concentrate on my homework, but there was too much going through my head.

Although my homework wasn't done, I closed my language arts book and stood in front of my mirror. I studied myself from head to toe, the way Ava had done the previous week. I didn't have the nerve to look at myself in my underwear.

I made a mental note of everything that was wrong with me. My hair was too thick and curly. I wondered why it couldn't be straight, fine, and silky like Ava's. Everyone admired her hair. I was too tall for a girl. There were some boys taller than me, but not many. Most boys wouldn't date girls taller than they were. My shoulders were too broad, not small and dainty like my friends. They were tiny and petite and people thought that was cute. No one thought that broad shoulders were cute.

After my shoulders, I looked at my chest. It was too big. I didn't like being an early bloomer. I didn't want people looking at my chest. I knew a lot of girls wanted what I had, but I didn't.

My legs were too thick. They were great for football and kicking the soccer ball around, but I wanted long, slender legs that would look good in dresses whenever I decided to wear them. Lastly, my feet were much too big. I was the only one of my friends who wore a size ten shoe. I could have probably found some other things wrong, but by then my vision had been blurred with tears and I couldn't see myself any longer.

I climbed up to my bed and slept until Aunt Jeanie called me down for dinner.

Norma served us all small bowls of Caesar salad, which I nibbled on. I was starving, but I needed to make this bowl of salad last throughout dinner time. When Norma came to collect our salad bowls, I told her not to take mine. When she brought the main course, lasagna, I declined.

Aunt Jeanie raised one eyebrow at me. "Bex, you have to eat."

"I am eating. This salad. I'm full." The lasagna smelled heavenly and my mouth watered from the aroma.

"You can't just eat that," Aunt Jeanie said. The other kids and Uncle Bob stopped eating and stared at me.

"You're the one who's always telling me that I eat too much and I need to go on a diet. I thought you'd be happy."

Aunt Jeanie's eyes grew wide. "Bex, I have never said such a thing. Do I encourage you to eat healthy and organic? Yes. I have never once suggested that you shouldn't eat."

"Well, I'm putting myself on a diet and I'm full from this salad," I lied. I was starving. I didn't see how Ava could stand a no-food diet.

"Why, Bex?" Ray asked.

"I'm changing my image."

Uncle Bob picked his fork back up again. "Why would you want to do that?"

Everyone looked at me expectantly, waiting for an answer. "Because I'm hideous!" I wailed. I totally did not mean to cry. I had been holding so much in all day and it was all coming out.

"What?" Aunt Jeanie asked.

I pushed my seat away from the table. "I'm big and ugly and made wrong. I'm a monster!" I ran from the table and up the stairs before anyone could say anything else.

Laying my head on my desk, I cried until I couldn't cry anymore. I thought about how stupid I was to tell those girls that the blog was no big deal. It was a huge deal and was making me second-guess myself. There was a light knock on the door.

"Bex, may I come in?" Aunt Jeanie asked.

I didn't answer. She was going to come in no matter what I said.

I sat up and wiped the tears from my face as she entered.

"What on earth was that about?" asked Aunt Jeanie as she took a chair that sat in the corner of my room and brought it next to me.

I turned in my swivel chair to face her. "I'm fat."

"What?"

"I'm fat, Aunt Jeanie. Don't act like you don't know."

She stared hard at me. "Bex, one thing I've always known about you was that you were comfortable in your own skin. Your size has never bothered you before. You've always told me that you liked the way you were. What's changed?"

I shrugged. I didn't want to tell her about the blog. It was too embarrassing.

"Bex," she urged.

"Okay, this kid at school started a blog where he rated how girls looked with a report card. On mine he said I should lose twenty pounds."

Aunt Jeanie closed her eyes and shook her head. "Bex, are you telling me that you let one silly boy shake your confidence?"

"He only said what everyone else is thinking." All the years of being called Big Red and Big Bex were catching up to me.

"Go stand in front of the mirror," Aunt Jeanie ordered.

"No," I replied. I couldn't look at myself anymore.

"Bex, do it," she said firmly.

Reluctantly, I rose and went over to the mirror. Aunt Jeanie stood behind me and pulled my hair back. I closed my eyes. The last thing I wanted to do was look at myself.

"Open your eyes, Bex."

I opened them. I saw the same old Bex that I always saw. I'd never thought anything was wrong with me. Sure I was taller than most girls, but I'd learned to live with that. But I had been wrong. Something was wrong with my size, right?

Aunt Jeanie rested her hands on my shoulders. "Your body is perfect just the way it is because it's your body. Think of all the things you do with it. You excel in basketball and soccer and lots of other sports. You run fast. There's nothing wrong with a body that can do all that."

"Yeah," I admitted. "That's true."

"Bex, tell me the name of a woman you really love— besides me. "Okay. Nana."

Aunt Jeanie turned me around so that I was facing her. "Why do you love her?"

"Because she loves me and she took care of me and Ray for a long time. She makes me feel good about who I am."

"Good," Aunt Jeanie said. "Name another."

"Aunt Alice because she's lots of fun and I can talk to her about almost anything, like a big sister."

Aunt Jeanie nodded. "Of all the things you listed, did you mention anything about the way they look?"

"No, I didn't."

She touched my shoulders again. "Because it doesn't matter. The things you mentioned tell what kind of people they are. You need to hold your head high and have confidence in yourself as a person. You're such a cute girl, Bex. You really are. There are just some things about you that you can't change, but you can change your attitude about them. That starts inside of you with self-respect. I want you to focus on health, not a size, and don't compare yourself to anyone else."

This was a lot coming from Aunt Jeanie who usually criticized everything about me.

"No, you're not a stick-thin girl, but so what? You're just the size you're supposed to be- not too big, but not too small either."

She was right. I'd always thought of myself as being at that happy medium.

Aunt Jeanie stepped away from me. "Bex, I know in the past I've been—critical." Sure, if that's the way she wants to say it. "It was never my intention to make you feel bad about yourself. You are beautiful just the way you are and I mean that."

She had said plenty of things that had made me feel that she was criticizing my looks, but I would ignore them and push her comments away. Why had Brayden's words hurt me so much more? Was it because he was a boy? I figured it was and also because he had broadcast his opinion of my appearance to the whole school. That part embarrassed me.

"Okay?" Aunt Jeanie asked.

I did feel a tiny little bit better.

"Now, let's go back down to dinner. What I won't do is allow you to starve yourself."

I nodded and followed her back to the dining room because I was starving. I didn't think there was any way I could starve myself, even if I wanted to. I had to eat.

That night I had a Skype conference call with my friends. I apologized for dismissing their concerns earlier, now that I knew what it felt like to have a boy point out what he felt was your flaw. They said more nice things to me like Aunt Jeanie had and I felt a lot better. I only hoped that other girls had people who loved them who could tell them how beautiful they were.

12

Meeting With the Enemy
#TeamFabulous

The following morning the eighth-grade girls met in the auditorium while the boys met in the gym. The eighth-grade teachers were all there since our first-period classes had been cancelled for the meeting.

Mrs. Conway took to the podium. "First and foremost, I would like to say that both blogs have been shut down and their creators will be suspended for the next week. Any more that crop up will be shut down and the perpetrators will be punished more harshly. This school has a zero-tolerance bullying policy." I breathed a sigh of relief. "With that being said, we thought you girls could benefit from a discussion about self-image and confidence."

Some of the girls groaned, but we needed it. Aunt Jeanie was right. We shouldn't have let one boy and his blog make us feel bad about ourselves.

Ms. Henry took the mike. "We're going to do an activity called Flower Petals. We're going to pass around some construction paper and I want each of you to take a sheet."

Several teachers passed around stacks of construction paper while Ms. Henry gave her instructions. "You will cut out a circle and write your name on it. That will be the center of your flower. Then you will create flower petals to glue on the outside."

Once we had our construction paper, we moved to the floor and sat in small groups, sharing glue and scissors. I felt like I was in elementary school all over again and I wasn't sure where our teachers where going with this arts and crafts project.

I'd chosen a sheet of yellow paper since yellow is one of my favorite colors. I followed Ms. Henry's instructions and formed a perfectly adequate flower, in my opinion.

Once we had finished creating our flowers, Mrs. Conway directed us to sit in small circles around the auditorium. After we had formed groups of eight, Mrs. Conway gave her next instructions.

"Now, you will pass your flower around your circle. Once you receive a girl's flower, I'd like you to write a compliment on one of the petals."

We passed our flowers around. I knew all of the girls in my circle except for one. One of the girls was Kristen Lee, whom I did not have a good history with. She was a rival of Ava G.'s and somehow I had gotten stuck in the middle of one of their fights. Other than that, finding compliments for the rest of the girls would be easy. I wrote nice thing on each flower I received.

On Chrissy Donnelly's I wrote, "She always helps me out in math class. It's nice of her because she doesn't have to do it." Math is a subject I struggle with. She helps me out when she can and she's very patient.

On Ashley Marra's flower, "She always gives great advice." It was true. Ashley's advice was almost motherly. She'd never given me any personal advice, but she wrote the advice column for the school paper and I found her guidance always to be spot on.

Someone passed me the flower of the one girl I didn't know. The name Rayna was written in the center of her lavender flower. She was wearing a really nice blouse, so I wrote that as my compliment. I felt guilty about not being able to write something deeper, but I didn't know the girl.

Kristen Lee's was going to be the real challenge for me. I thought for a long moment. The girl sitting next to me was waiting for me to pass the flower on. I decided to go with. "Kristen is great at karate." I should know. I had once been the unfortunate recipient of one of her powerful kicks.

When I got my flower back, I was a little nervous about reading what the girls had written. I wasn't sure what to expect. I read all seven of my comments:

"Bex is very clever. She thinks of things no one else thinks of." That wasn't always a good thing.

"Bex tries really hard. Math is not her best subject, but she never gives up."

"She's a great leader."

"Bex is a great friend. She always sticks up for hers."

"She's great at sports. Better than most boys I know."

"She's super funny. She always makes me laugh when I'm in a bad mood."

"Bex marches to her own drum." That was a compliment, wasn't it?

"Bex stands up for what she believes in, even if no one else does."

Huh. I've never even realized some of those things about myself. As corny as this activity had seemed, I kind of felt like I was sitting on top of the world at that moment. As I looked around my circle, I could tell that the other girls were pleased also. Smiles all around.

Next, we made three larger circles. In this circle we had to give compliments to the girls on the left and right of us. We had to give them two compliments, one about their personality and one about their physical appearance. When I looked down at my flower, I realized that none of the compliments there had anything to do with the way I looked. There were many other things about me that people noticed.

Leslie Carpenter gave me my first compliment. I'd known Leslie since the first grade, but we'd never really hung out outside of class. "What I like about Bex is that she doesn't care what people say about her. Everything rolls right off her back." If only she knew. I looked at Leslie and she smiled. "She's confident enough in herself not to believe what people say about her."

I had been that way, usually. But lately, I had been letting comments get to me.

Leslie continued on with her second compliment. "And I think Bex is adorable. Really, I've always thought she was cute."

"Thanks," I muttered.

When we were done with that exercise, Mrs. Conway called us back to the seats. She talked to us about self-image and how we needed to focus on the great things about ourselves.

"One of the major concerns I have is girls possibly developing poor eating habits, like not eating enough. That is a horrible thing to do to your bodies. Not eating slows down your heart and blood pressure. You'll lose muscle and your body will go through weakness and fatigue. You might experience kidney failure and dry skin and hair loss, among other things." She talked some more about being healthy and we did an exercise where we learned to appreciate our bodies.

I couldn't see any of the Avas from where I was sitting, but I hoped they were listening and taking Mrs. Conway's words seriously.

I knew I definitely felt better and I knew the other girls did, but I wondered how long that would last. After all, it was just one conversation and we were bombarded everyday with influences telling us that we weren't good enough. Mrs. Conway said that she planned on making things like this part of her regular curriculum and I thought it was a great idea. We all chanted "Team Fabulous" on the count of three.

When we were done, Ms. Henry announced that we would be joining the boys in the gymnasium. I wasn't looking forward to that at all.

Leslie walked beside me as we made our way to the gym. "I wonder what they were talking to the boys about. How not to be judgmental, rude jerks?"

I shrugged. I had no idea what they could have been talking to the boys about. As far as I knew, they were just fine with their looks.

Leading the pack of girls, I was one of the first to enter the gymnasium. I stopped in my tracks when the boys stood and applauded. Mr. Hawthorne and Principal Radcliff motioned for us to keep walking and to have a seat on the bleachers. The boys didn't sit down or stop clapping until we were all seated and that took a while. I was thoroughly confused.

Principal Radcliff took a microphone and stood in the middle of the gym floor. "Ladies, I know you may not understand why the boys just did what they did, so maybe one of them should explain." Principal Radcliff pointed at someone and Brayden stood up and took the mike.

"Hi. We had a long discussion on how to treat girls and what girls think, and we wanted to show that we celebrate and respect you. Look, I'm really sorry about the things I put in my blog and the things I said. I wouldn't want anyone to do or say those things to my mom or sister."

I was stunned. I had never heard Brayden say anything so nice. It made me wonder what kind of conversation they had had.

We had a group discussion about our boy-girl war. It turns out we girls weren't exactly innocent in all this. We had judged the boys also. Even when Brayden and a group of boys were being jerks, we'd thrown all the boys in that same category, which wasn't fair. Besides that, it wasn't very nice to tell boys they were only useful for grunt work and killing disgusting creatures.

Anybody who wanted to talk got a chance to go up to the mike. We stayed there until lunchtime. We had learned nothing academic that morning, but we'd gotten a lesson that could last a lifetime.

13

Making Up
—feeling relieved ☺

That evening, I sat on the front porch cleaning my soccer cleats. I sighed when Santiago walked up the sidewalk carrying his backpack. Even though we'd made a breakthrough during the meeting, I hadn't spoken to Santiago all day and I didn't feel like fighting.

I slid over on the top step so that he could have a seat. He sat down and pulled a laptop from his backpack.

"What are you doing?"

"Cleaning my cleats."

"Oh."

A long awkward silence followed. My cleats were clean, but I continued to wipe them out of lack of anything else to do. "What are you doing here?" I asked finally.

Santiago lifted the lid of his laptop and began to type. "I wanted to say sorry. For the things I said. The way I acted. Especially what I said about your parents. I was way out of line."

"Okay. I'm sorry for blaming you for how Brayden and some of the other guys were acting. That wasn't your fault."

Santiago nodded. "I accept your apology." We smiled at each other and then looked away. "You know," Santiago continued, "I know you think it's crazy, but I kind of miss Sookie."

I laughed. "I kind of miss complaining about having to carry her around. I can't believe Mrs. Conway gave us all C's for destroying our babies."

"I think we got off easy. We shouldn't have taken our anger out on the kids."

I looked at Santiago and he burst out laughing. Thank goodness, he was only joking.

"Bex, I wanted to show you something." He handed me his laptop.

I looked at the screen and a sick feeling hit my chest. "This is Brayden's blog. Principal Radcliff shut it down. Why is it up again?"

"I put it back up."

I gave him the side eye. "What?"

"You know you're talking to a technological genius here."

"I know. I know you *can* get a site back up, but the question is *why* would you do that?"

"I wanted to make one last post and then I'll shut it down for good. Read it."

I looked at the screen.

Santiago's Report Card
Student: Bex Carter
Subjects:
Personality: A
Awesomeness: A
Brains: A
Humor: A

Beauty: A
Overall: Excellent
Comments: Bex is one of the coolest girls I know. The last thing she should be worried about is what some stupid guys think of her.
Recommendations: She shouldn't change a thing.

I felt a tear slide down my cheek and I wiped it away quickly.

"Are you crying?"

"Of course not. It's hot. I'm sweating."

"From your eyeballs?"

I looked at Santiago and smiled. "This is really sweet, Santiago." I handed him back his laptop. "Thanks so much."

"You're welcome. Like I said, I'll take the blog back down." He stuffed his laptop into his backpack and stood up.

I stood up too. "Uh, maybe you can keep that up for a little while."

"Sure, Bex." He slid the straps of his backpack on his shoulders and started down the walkway.

"Santiago?"

He stopped and turned around. "Yeah?"

"Did you really mean that stuff or were you just trying to make me feel better?"

"Both."

I nodded. Santiago stood there looking like he wanted to say something else, then he thought better of it. "Bye, Bex."

"Bye, Santiago."

I watched him walk down the sidewalk and away from Aunt Jeanie's house.

A week later, things seemed to be back to normal at school. There were no flour-babies, boys and girls were speaking to each other, and no one was worried about being humiliated by some hot-not list. The only thing that was abnormal was Brayden Avery standing in front of my locker. He and Ava had just returned from their suspensions.

"H-hey, Bex. What's up?"

"I should be asking you that question. What do you want?"

"I wanted to give you a personal apology. It was rotten of me to do what I did. I was really wrong for pushing you. You can punch me in the face if you want." I was tempted, but I declined. "I hope you can forgive me and be a better person than me and not show anyone that picture."

I frowned. "What picture?"

"You know. Ava told me. Don't make me say it, please." He began to back away from me like he was afraid and I was confused. "I'm sorry. See you around."

I pulled my language arts book from my locker and went to find Ava. As I suspected, she was in the girls' bathroom by the auditorium with the other Avas, planted in front of the mirror.

"Ava, can I talk to you?" I asked, pulling her to the side.

"Bex, I should clarify in case you haven't realized it, but our truce is officially over. You really shouldn't be talking to me."

I rolled my eyes. "Why did Brayden just beg me not to release some picture?"

Ava's eyes widened. "Oh, that? See, I took a picture of Brayden's foot. I knew it might come in handy one day. I told him that I sent it to your phone and that you had the power to send it to the whole school if he messed with you again."

"But I don't have a phone."

Ava shrugged. "He doesn't know that. But now for as long as you know him, you'll have this to hold over his head. Just say the word and I'll release it."

I was caught a little off guard. It wasn't every day that Ava did something nice for me. I could get used to that.

Everyone was still calling Brayden E.T. and making alien noises when he walked by, so I figured he'd been punished enough.

"I don't think that will be necessary."

Ava flipped her hair over her shoulder. "Suit yourself. Anyway, like I said, the truce is over." She strolled back over to her place in front of the mirror.

"I heard you. I heard you." Yes, things were definitely back to normal.

Mrs. Conway rescheduled our dinner party for Friday night. At first she had cancelled it for our poor behavior, but then she decided that we would learn more by having it.

She'd made a rule that we had to sit next to our partners from the Family Living project.

The dinner was catered by a nearby restaurant, but the boys served the girls dinner, which was really nice.

Santiago placed a plate in front of me. "Thanks, Santiago."

"No problem," he said, sitting beside me. He looked down at the plate of chicken fingers, mashed potatoes, and salad. "Are we good?"

I scooped up a spoonful of mashed potatoes. "Of course. We've been friends for a long time. Friends fight sometimes."

"Yeah, especially when one friend is being a colossal jerk."

"It's okay. We're good now."

"I had been dreading this project," Santiago said, "but I have to admit that I learned a lot. Do you miss Sookie?"

"Not at all." As far as I knew, Santiago had Sookie sitting on his dresser at home as some kind of souvenir. Weird.

Santiago laughed and raised his cup of punch. "Here's to friends forever, no matter what."

I touched my glass of punch against his. "No matter what."

After that, the girls served dessert, which ended up being my favorite thing—red velvet cake! So, maybe Mrs. Conway's project wasn't as bad as I had thought it would be. It was definitely a learning experience. Well played, Mrs. Conway. Well played.

Family Living Assignment Wrap-Up
Question:
What are you taking away from this project?

Bex: Having a family and planning for the future is hard work and you have to learn to compromise. You will fight sometimes, but you need to find a way to work it out.

Santiago: I learned that I'm not always right and there's no such thing as woman's work. Both people have to do their part to make a family work. It also helps being married to someone you like—someone you're friends with.

Life lesson from Bex: Love yourself no matter what anybody says. Remember, the ones who are criticizing you aren't perfect themselves.

Keep Reading for a Sneak Peek of Love, Politics, and Red Velvet Cupcakes (Book 5 of the Bex Carter Series)

Chirpy grabbed the flyer with the requirements. "Okay, the responsibilities of the president are—"

"Pass. What's next?"

"Okay. The vice president—"

"Chirpy! Everyone knows the v.p. does more work than the president. They're like the president's slave."

Chirpy sighed. "All right, all right. Secretary. The responsibility of the class secretary are to attend all meeting and take thorough notes."

"No," I said.

"What do you mean no? That sounds easy."

"Chirpy, my hand will cramp up and I would have to pay attention to take good notes. Do you have any idea how boring a student council meeting is? I'm not going to be able to pay attention."

"Bex, have you even been to a student council meeting?"

"No."

"Then how do you know they're boring?"

"I just knoooow. Trust me. What else is there?"

"Treasurer, but you're not that good with math."

"Chirpy, it's just counting money. I can add," I said.

"Okay. The class treasurer is responsible for collecting money for the seventh grade account and keeping a running tally of gains and expenditures."

Me and money got along fine. I could totally do that.

"The treasurer is also responsible for organizing events and fundraisers—"

"Next!"

"Bex, come on. None of these jobs is going to be easy."

"Chirpy, you and I both know that anything I try to organize is going to turn out to be a disaster."

"Okay, the last job is class recorder. The class recorder's responsibilities are to read the minutes from the last meeting and to make sure the meetings start and end on time."

I waited for her to finish reading the list. "Is that it?"

Chirpy shrugged. "Yeah, that's all it says."

I sat up. "That's it! That's the perfect job for me. Bex Carter is running for eighth grade class recorder, the easiest job there is."

Chirpy shook her head. "Shoot for the stars, Bex. Shoot for the stars."

The following day anyone who wanted to run for a position on the student council had to report to Mr. Hall's classroom after school. There were about twenty-five kids in the room. I wondered how many were running for class recorder. I just had to get that position. My social studies grade and a super-cool cell phone were at stake.

Just as the meeting was about to begin, someone took a seat at the desk behind me. The smell of evil almost overpowered my senses. I didn't have to turn around to know that it was Ava G. I rolled my eyes and prayed for the meeting to begin before she could say anything to me.

Mr. Hall stood at his podium with a pen. "Good afternoon ladies and gentlemen. It's nice to see so many of you eager to participate in student government.We'll start with the position of class recorder," he announced. "Who's interested in running?"

Me, a girl, and a boy raised our hands. Ava laughed behind me.

"At least you know what position losers are supposed to run for."

I turned to her. "It's not a loser position. It's a very important position."

"Yeah? Then how come only Scary Sherry and Frog Boy will be running against you? You know that's the only way you'll win, by running against bigger losers than you."

"I'm not a loser and you better stop calling me that. I'm a *winner*."

"No, Bex. I'm a winner. Watch me win this election. I'm going to be president and I'm going to make your life miserable."

"Yeah?"

"Yeah."

I turned around quickly and before I could even think about what I was saying I blurted out, "Mr. Hall, scratch that. I'm going to be running for president instead."

Somebody should really tape my mouth shut.

CPSIA information can be obtained at www.ICGtesting.com
Printed in the USA
LVOW12s1818200814

400097LV00011B/1088/P